STYLE & MANORS

STYLE & MANORS

A charming and amusing account of life on a Suffolk estate. Continuing his memoirs of his time on Sir Charles Buckley's estate, James Aden deals with obstacles from the discovery of Roman treasure to the tramp living in the attic of Frampton Hall; he finds his day varied, especially with the arrival of Sir Charles's heir, Sebastian who provides him with insights into the life of the traditional landed estates as they slowly come to terms with the twenty-first century.

STYLE
& MANORS

by

Rory Clark

Magna Large Print Books
Long Preston, North Yorkshire,
BD23 4ND, England.

British Library Cataloguing in Publication Data.

Clark, Rory
    Style & manors.

    A catalogue record of this book is
    available from the British Library

    ISBN   978-0-7505-3841-1

First published in Great Britain by Robinson,
an imprint of Constable & Robinson Ltd., 2013

Copyright © Rory Clark, 2013

Cover illustration by arrangement with Constable & Robinson Ltd.

The right of Rory Clark to be identified as the author of this work has
been asserted by him in accordance with the Copyright, Designs and
Patents Act, 1988

Published in Large Print 2014 by arrangement with
Constable & Robinson Ltd.

Magna Large Print is an imprint of Library Magna Books Ltd.

Printed and bound in Great Britain by
T.J. (International) Ltd., Cornwall, PL28 8RW

To Rowan with love

My thanks to

Sue Hardwick for all her help but particularly typing and redrafting the book, to Ruth Tott, my publisher, for persuading me to write it and Hal Norman for editing once again.

Chapter 1

There was a dead ferret on my windscreen. Assuming it hadn't fallen out of the sky, somebody must have put it there. An attached note would have been helpful, but it lay quite alone beside the wiper-blade. It was rather pretty for a ferret, foxy brown with a white chest, but clearly dead, not just having a bit of a lie down.

The absence of further information led me to believe that this was all part of the ongoing battle between the estate's gamekeeper and our local poacher. Neither individual was likely to engage the law in resolving difficulties, both having been on the wrong side of it in the past. A less formal approach to Sir Charles' agent was more favourable. Hence the ferret on my car.

I turned around and walked back into the estate office.

'Oh, you're back quickly,' remarked Anne, my secretary.

'Yes,' I replied, 'there's a dead ferret on my car and I want to know who put it there.'

'There's a what?' she asked as I strode into my office and closed the door.

I picked up the telephone and dialled Tony Williams' number. He was the head keeper and might be able to shed some light on the situation.

His answerphone came on.

'That's Williams 'ere, I'm out,' it said. Beep...

A not very enticing encouragement to leaving a message I thought and rang his mobile.

''Ello,' he answered, amongst a buzz of crackles.

'Tony, it's James Aden here,' I replied. 'Have you got a minute?' There was a silence, some more buzzing and a slightly clearer voice said, 'I'll go up the 'ill, 'old on, Mr Aden.'

I could hear him stomping through the undergrowth as he made his way to better reception and reflected on Sir Charles' views towards 'telegraphies' as he called them. Not only did Sir Charles not have a mobile phone, he only had two proper telephones in his house, and his house was the size of a small village. However, his stringencies did not extend to his staff.

'I'm 'ere now, can you 'ar me?'

'Ah yes, that's better Tony.' I explained about the ferret.

'That'll be that damn Thorpe I've no doubt,' he said. 'He's a bloody fool 'e is.'

'Well, we've got to sort this business out,' I said. 'He's taken an awkward line with the estate ever since he was ousted from the Frampton Ferret Society. Can you come in and discuss it later this afternoon?'

'Bloody fool,' he repeated, presumably still referring to Thorpe. 'I'll be back in about fourish then.' With that the line went dead.

'I'm off again now,' I told Anne, 'be back by four. Tony Williams is due in then.'

I walked back to my car, parked outside the estate office in the village square. The ferret hadn't moved so I flung it on the passenger seat and got in beside it. I was due up at the Hall to see Sir Charles for my weekly meeting.

Although we saw or spoke to each other most days, Sir Charles had decided early on in our working relationship that an agenda and weekly meeting was the professional way forward.

In a way it was but as we tended to discuss estate matters most days compiling the agenda was, at times, a little awkward. Frankly, often all it could read was:

Those present (him and me)
Matters outstanding (none)
Date of next meeting

I did what I could to expand on this.

This afternoon's matters included: venison distribution, Eastern Shires' proposals to replace the village sewer (no connection between the two items), Miss Cartwright's unexpected baby and redecorating the estate office.

I pulled up outside the back door on the East Front of Frampton Hall and let myself into the servants' quarters.

'Ah, Mr Aden, Sir Charles is expecting you,' stated Hole, the butler. 'Please follow me and I'll show you through.'

I knew the house as well as he did but the formality never wavered. We arrived at Sir Charles' study some while later, whereupon Hole knocked loudly on the door before opening it.

Sir Charles was deeply engaged in poking the fire, his tweed-clad bottom welcoming us.

'Ah, James,' he said, glancing up. 'This bloody sycamore is a devil to get going. Not dry enough,

13

still green.' I wasn't sure why, with 1,000 acres of woodland, the foresters had sent it down to the Hall. There must have been some seasoned logs somewhere. I would make enquiries.

He stood up and went over to his huge mahogany partner's desk positioned in front of the bay window, overlooking the 300 acres of parkland in front of the house.

Hole left, gently closing the door behind him.

'We'll get some better firewood up here Sir Charles,' I said. 'There's plenty of decent stuff available.'

'Jolly good, I'll leave it to you James,' he replied. 'Now take that seat and we'll have a look at the agenda.'

He fumbled about on his desk and found the relevant piece of paper whilst I perched in an elegant but uncomfortable Louis XV occasional chair which was missing a castor.

'I see,' he exclaimed, 'the venison.'

'Yes,' I said, the chair wobbling at my slightest movement. Each year the estate gave a haunch of venison to all its employees, and more controversially to some of the tenants. 'I thought it would be useful to reconsider the tenants' list, Sir Charles,' I continued. 'Remember last year there was a bit of a fuss over some people being on it, with others left off.'

'Damn bloody annoying, all that business,' he retorted, 'it's my venison to give to whom I like.'

'I agree Sir Charles, but I think, for instance, that it was unfortunate we sent a haunch to Miss Styles. She's not only a vegetarian but an avid opponent of shooting deer.'

'That was unfortunate,' he agreed, 'and a bloody waste. I don't know how she got on the list.'

'I think it was probably because we used to send some to the people who lived in her cottage previously,' I ventured. 'However, perhaps I could prepare an updated list for you to consider?'

'I think so, I think so,' he agreed. 'Yes it's time to revise it. Just my meat-eating tenants, employees and the village poor.'

Those criteria in themselves, I thought, were hardly going to make matters better. Miss Styles we now knew was a vegetarian, but I thought it unlikely that we would be able to draw up a comprehensive list of the vegetarians who resided on Sir Charles' property. Furthermore, whether some people would like to be considered as the village poor was another issue.

'Now the second thing here,' went on Sir Charles, 'is the sewer. What's the matter with it?'

'We've had notice from Eastern Shires that it's collapsing in the High Street, so they are going to replace the whole length, Sir Charles. From the post office down to the pub.'

'I see,' Sir Charles said, 'and when is this disturbance taking place? Not over Christmas surely? And don't forget we've got the street fair on the twelfth of December.'

'No, they are starting at the end of January, for eight weeks I'm told.'

'Well, we'll just have to put up with it, I suppose. I have to say that it doesn't seem that long ago since they put it in. It hasn't lasted very well.'

I could sense we were about to slide back in time as Sir Charles reminisced about his early

15

years on the Estate. He had been born in Frampton Hall seventy-five years ago, and despite various absences for school, war and travelling, had a full and enthusiastic knowledge of local history. The estate was, after all, his life.

'It wasn't until after the war they put the drains in,' he recounted. 'Up until then we were on the bucket and chuck-it system in most of the cottages.'

'Thank goodness we've moved on,' I remarked. '...perhaps we ought to move on with the agenda.'

'Indeed. Now Miss Cartwright's unexpected baby, it says here,' he said, looking down at his piece of paper. 'What's this about?'

Katy Cartwright was the sixteen-year-old daughter of the village baker and his wife. Inevitably there had been some unkind remarks about buns in the oven and so on, but the truth was it had caused a family crisis.

Sir Charles took the responsibilities of his huge estate very seriously and was well aware that not only did he own most of the property in the area, but also that many families' livelihoods depended on his concerns. He viewed his position almost as a private welfare state.

Katy Cartwright, barely out of school, was an intelligent and attractive girl who had got involved with a somewhat unpleasant (as it turned out) lad from the nearby town of Bury St Edmunds.

'You'll remember Katy Cartwright, Sir Charles,' I suggested, 'she's the eldest of the Cartwright daughters and helps in the shop on Saturdays.'

'Yes, I do,' he said. 'Tall, willowy girl with extremely long blonde hair. Very attractive young

16

thing I always think. Oh, dear, she's got into trouble then?'

'It seems so, Sir Charles. She's expecting this baby in a couple of months now and the father's not interested, leaving her with her family in the flat above the bakery. You can imagine they're deeply upset by the whole thing and I wondered what you might think of trying to find her a cottage?'

'Well you know I'm all for keeping our young people in the village,' he said, 'but surely the lad can't just bugger orf? Damned disgrace if you ask me.'

'Well I'm afraid he has just buggered off,' I confirmed. 'They might get him to pay towards looking after the baby, but even that's unlikely. Anyway I felt I should bring it to your attention.'

'I'm glad you did, thank you James. There's no question, we'll have to help. The Cartwrights have been in this village for over 100 years. We have a duty to help, but have we got any empty cottages at the moment?'

'Unfortunately we don't have any vacant, but there is a little flat over the stables behind the post office. I would imagine that that might be suitable for now,' I suggested.

'Oh, yes, I know the place. Is it big enough?' he asked.

'It's got two bedrooms and a sort of living room-cum-kitchen,' I explained, 'and frankly it's either that or move into council accommodation in the town. It would be impossible for her to stay at home.'

'I wouldn't have thought she would want one of

17

those council places,' Sir Charles said, pushing back in his chair. 'Bloody concrete rabbit warrens designed to drive the occupants into lives of corruption and disease,' he added.

'Well,' I said, 'I don't quite know whether they are that bad Sir Charles, but I know what you mean.'

'Offer her that flat straight away,' he butted in, 'it's what we're here for. No doubt the council will pay her bills, like they do for half the country. Do ask Miss Cartwright if she would like to have a look round.'

'Very good, Sir Charles. I'll arrange to see the Cartwrights this afternoon.'

The final item on the agenda was merely to mention that the interior of the estate office was to be decorated the following week, possibly causing some disruption.

'Good, good,' he said, 'keep it looking smart. It's the public face of the estate and I always say it's what everyone remembers us by.'

I thought it highly unlikely that anyone remembered the estate by the interior of our offices. The massive grandeur of the stately pile, Frampton Hall, set in its acres of rolling parkland, or indeed the largely preserved medieval village of Frampton, would have sprung to my mind. However, if Sir Charles thought otherwise, so be it.

'And don't forget to use estate green in the lavatory,' he remarked, 'a most relaxing colour that I use in all the loos in this house.'

'No, I hadn't forgotten,' I assured him, as despite the fact that I didn't particularly want our visitors relaxing in the office lavatory, I knew Sir

Charles' particular views on the matter.

I left him in his study and strode briskly along the labyrinth of freezing cold corridors towards the East Wing. I always marvelled at the size of the house and dwelt for a moment on the bizarre fact that no one seemed to know how many rooms it contained. One day I would count them. I had tried once but had been interrupted by the housekeeper when in the fortieth bedroom, and then lost count due to her insistence that I should inspect a leaking pipe.

Hole came out of his pantry as I walked past.

'Ah, Mr Aden,' he said, halting my progress. 'We've taken a call for you from the estate office. Your secretary has asked that you telephone her before leaving the Hall.'

He showed me through to his office from where the considerable affairs of the household were managed. A small log fire was burning in the grate and a faint aroma of pipe tobacco hung in the air. Hole was a keen pipe smoker with an admirable collection of pipes set out in a holder on his desk. Organised and regimented, it was like his command of the household.

His office was lined with shelves. Some contained books which were mainly of reference or instruction. One that particularly drew my attention was entitled *A Gentleman's Guide to the Upkeep and Maintenance of Hunting Boots*. It wasn't the content that intrigued me so much as how the author had unearthed enough material to fill a whole book. Other shelves were taken up by the pieces of equipment he needed to carry out his butlering tasks around the house. There were candles, brushes, tongs, Sir Charles' cellar list and much more besides. All useful no doubt but one fact stood out. Everything was old fashioned. There was no computer, fax machine, or mobile phone. There was however a manual Olympia typewriter and a Bakelite telephone.

He beckoned me to the telephone, adding, 'Please do telephone the estate office.'

I noticed that the number on the piece of paper in the middle of the dial still read Frampton 2, which reminded me of my suggestion a year or so previously that we install broadband in the Hall.

To be fair I had suggested it half-heartedly, realising that neither Sir Charles nor Hole would have had much interest in it. But I felt that they should at least consider the option.

It had been clear from the outset that it was a nonstarter. The internet had drawn murmurs of recognition, but the idea of broadband had become so bogged down with confusion about broad beans and elastic bands that I had aborted the discussion at an early stage.

I picked up the phone and dialled the office.

'James here,' I said, 'I gather you rang me?'

'Oh, yes,' replied Anne, my secretary. 'The garage has been on about Sir Charles' car and the MOT. Apparently it needs two tyres and they need to know whether to fit new ones or remoulds?'

'He always has remoulds Anne, tell them to carry on as usual.'

I had become used to the peculiar frugalities of the baronet's lifestyle. An individual probably worth well over £100 million worrying about the

20

cost of his car tyres had initially seemed in-
conceivable, but to me now it was just part of the
job.

Chapter 2

The job was managing the 10,000 acres of Sir Charles Buckley's Frampton Hall Estate. It encompassed a stately pile, a complete village, dozens of farms and a sizeable, somewhat eclectic estate staff. I had been offered the job soon after moving to Suffolk with my wife Sophie a couple of years earlier. She had inherited a small farm from her uncle, which had decided our course of action. Sophie ran the farm with the help of a couple of elderly farm workers and a housekeeper, whilst I worked as the resident agent for Sir Charles.

It was an unusual job and it meant having to turn one's mind to the huge variety of matters that arose within the estate's community – from agricultural law to rudimentary plumbing, local politics to pheasant rearing, forestry management to organising the village fete.

One afternoon I was in the office daydreaming about how fortunate I was to have such a wonderful job and how lucky I was not to have to fight my way into a big city every day. Just how different my job was to what might have been was brought home to me one morning when I caught the 7.24 am Colchester to London train.

I had a meeting with the estate lawyers in their London offices. Although I preferred travelling by car the nightmare of tackling the A12 into the city at rush hour outweighed the inconvenience of public transport.

The train was ten minutes late to the platform so before I had even embarked I was irritated. As it drew to a stop I was propelled by a crowd of commuters through the door into a packed carriage. All the seats were occupied so I stood squashed with others in the aisle. For many it must have been the usual journey. They balanced against the swaying of the train reading newspapers seemingly oblivious to the discomfort. I had purchased a paper but without the perfected skills acquired by practice there was no way I could read it. Instead, I concentrated on standing upright and studiously avoided eye contact with the people next to me. As we approached Shenfield an obnoxious smell pervaded the area around me. I am sure that it had nothing to do with Shenfield but rather a lot to do with the man standing beside me. I chanced a quick glance at him and unfortunately caught his eye. He didn't appear to acknowledge his misdemeanour but I reddened with unwarranted embarrassment. The woman on my other side glanced at me. Noticing my red face she must have immediately drawn the wrong conclusion, that I was responsible for the ghastly whiff. It was therefore with great discomfort that I continued the journey to London. Thank goodness my job didn't involve coping with this on a daily basis.

I was snapped out of my reverie by Anne who came to tell me that the head keeper was waiting in the estate office reception hall.

I walked out of my office to greet him.

'Tony, thanks for coming in,' I said, shaking his

callused hand. The effect of years of pulling pheasants' necks was evident.

'That's all right, Mr Aden,' he replied, crushing my hand. 'You got a problem with a ferret I 'ear.'

I went back into my office and offered him a seat. His large frame, clad in the estate tweed, dwarfed the chair. It creaked ominously as he sat down.

'Well, I found a ferret,' I explained, 'a dead one, on my car. But I have to say I think the problem's more yours than mine. I guess it's to do with this poaching business.'

Tony Williams chuckled slightly and scratched his ear.

'I dunno about that, Mr Aden,' he said, 'it's 'ard to say without seeing the ferret.'

'Oh, come off it Tony, people don't just go around putting dead ferrets on other people's cars. It's bound to be Thorpe. Anyway I've got the ferret if that helps.'

'I grant you, Mr Aden, it possibly is Thorpe. But why he's put it on your car I dunno.'

'Presumably to draw me into your row. I need to know what's going on and then somehow we'll have to sort it out.'

The grapevine had alerted me to some skulduggery in the woods, but experience had taught me to avoid entanglement with keepers' affairs unless absolutely necessary. Clearly it was now absolutely necessary.

'Some buggers 'ave bin at Sir Charles' birds, that's what it's about. I've caught him up round the pens four times now and I'll swear he's had one or two in his bag. Course I couldn't prove it

24

unless I flattened the bloke and took his bag,' he gushed.

'No, don't do that,' I said. 'You'll end up in clink.'

'Tha's the trouble innit?' he continued. 'Can't touch the thieving bastard, the law don't wanna know, so I gave him a warning.'

'And what was that?'

'I'd let a ferret loose in his chick'n house.'

'And you did?'

'I reckon. See I caught him again so I kept my word.'

'And he found the ferret and shot it, I suppose?'

'Well, seems like it. Mind you, twas 'opeless animal, that one.'

I thought for a moment. Such disagreements within the village community were unfortunate, although not wholly unheard of, but rough tactics like this could escalate.

'We do have a card to play here,' I pondered. 'Unfortunately, Thorpe doesn't have an estate cottage, he lives in one of the council houses, as you know. But he does rent his allotment from us. Leave it to me.'

Tony didn't look all that reassured. He was all for personal confrontation, which he was good at, admittedly. I was better at negotiation.

As he left I called after him. 'By the way Tony, can you take the ferret please? It's on the front seat of my car.'

It was by now nearly 5 pm and it was one of those dark December days when people want to rush home to settle in front of the fire. I could hear the rest of the estate office staff getting ready to leave. Apart from Anne there was Gail the farm secretary and Brenda, who looked after the accounts.

At one second past five there was a collective shout of 'Goodnight', and the door slammed behind them. I too needed to be punctual this evening as I was expected home for an early supper. I was then going out to attend an evening meeting on 'Eco Building for Sustainable Development'.

Sophie and I lived at Cordwainers Hall, the 300-acre farm that Sophie had inherited from her uncle. It lay just off the Frampton Estate, a convenient ten-minute drive from the office.

'Hi, darling,' I shouted as I walked in through the back hall, 'where are you?'

'Hi, in here,' Sophie replied from the kitchen.

'Hello,' I said, giving her a kiss, 'had a good day?'

'Not bad thanks. Just pottering really, and took Emma out for a walk with the dogs. Damn cold though.'

Emma was lying in a basket on the kitchen table. A little four-month-old bundle of joy, or noise, I wasn't totally sure, asleep in the warmth of the kitchen.

I was about to pick her up for a hug when Sophie interrupted. 'Don't wake her, she's quiet at last. I've had her screaming on and off all day.'

'Oh, dear,' I said, dropping back. 'Well I certainly don't want to start her off again. I wonder why she's been so noisy – perhaps there is something wrong with her?'

We were both new to parenthood and the joys were tempered by a sense of not being entirely confident that we knew what we were doing. Delightful though Emma was, at times it could seem rather daunting and a tremendous responsibility.

So far, however, with a bit of natural instinct and a couple of books on the subject, it was going well.

'She's just grumpy,' Sophie continued. 'Anyway supper's ready so come and eat now because I know you have to go out soon.'

'Excellent, thanks. What is it?'

'It's the rest of the chicken casserole – it's in the Aga if you want to get it out.'

Rather hurriedly we ate our meal, thankful that Emma slept on, undisturbed by the delicious aroma of the food.

'Will you be late tonight?' asked Sophie.

'Oh, I hope not,' I replied, 'I don't particularly want to go at all but it's one of those things that I ought to do.'

'What a pain. It's such a miserable night out there.'

I only had to go to Bury St Edmunds so it wasn't that much of an ordeal. The subject itself was more of a trial, the meeting hall likely to be patronised by bearded men in sandals. However, the subject had some useful aspects worth considering and I knew that professionally I had to keep up to date with such topics.

Sustainable development has a huge role to play in our future and on the estate we were already engaged in several projects with others in the pipeline. However, it had long been my opinion that the green lobby really needed to rebrand itself. It was all very well harping on about vegetarianism, or moving to the Brecon Beacons to live in a hut fuelled by manure but the movement had to become more mainstream. To my surprise I was encouraged by the meeting. Despite the unnaturally large number of bearded sandal-wearers there appeared to be a good number of normal businesspeople and property owners taking an interest. I could not imagine any of them contemplating harvesting a beard which their wives could then knit into a pair of driving gloves.

No, it was much more businesslike with new ideas about energy-efficient property construction, ways of recycling materials and a lot of talk about carbon footprints. That was something I would need to read up on, partly as I hadn't got a clue what they were, and partly because I knew Sir Charles would only be persuaded to do anything about it if a good case was presented to him.

The meeting finished at 9.30 pm and I hurried away, declining the opportunity for a drink at the bar. There wasn't anyone there who I knew that well and I was keen to get home to see Sophie and the baby.

It was raining hard when I went outside, with a powerful wind also making driving conditions difficult. The flat, wild, arable land around Bury St Edmunds provided no shelter from the gales driving across from Siberia. Despite its uncluttered charm in the summer, Suffolk can be a mean, inhospitable county in the winter. We were fortunate in Frampton as it lay on the edge of the flatands, in an area of gently rolling hills which gave some relief from the harsh winds.

I took the main road out of town, peering intently through the rain hitting the windscreen. It was difficult to see clearly, especially when there was an oncoming car with dazzling headlights. It was at such a moment that I saw an animal on the verge. I couldn't quite make out what it was – fox size but the wrong colour. Much browner. A badger perhaps, but I didn't think so. I kept going for a few hundred yards before deciding that it was possibly a dog. If it was, I asked myself, what on earth was it doing there? I was puzzled and couldn't just leave it, not in this terrible weather at the side of a busy road. Whatever it was it would get killed.

I turned my Land Rover around and headed back to where I thought I had seen it. I pulled into a mini lay-by adjoining a field gate and got out of the car. Fortunately I had a torch but I was only wearing a light coat that did nothing to keep out the rain. I crossed the road, dodging the oncoming traffic, and wandered slowly back along the verge.

Initially I couldn't find anything. Perhaps it was further back than I remembered, or indeed it had been a fox that was now two or three fields away.

I felt a bit foolish, not to mention freezing cold and wet, and started back to the Land Rover. It was as I swung the torch round that I saw it. Half hidden under the hedge was a bedraggled, frightened small brown dog, its terrified eyes reflected by the glare of my torch.

I lowered the light so it could see me. I had no idea whether it would be friendly or not, so I cautiously crouched down and beckoned it towards me. The poor little thing didn't move.

'Come on, little dog,' I said, 'you shouldn't be out here.'

I kept talking to it, gradually moved closer. It didn't come out from the hedge, but neither did it appear alarmed. I could see now that it was wearing a collar and looked like a border terrier. Eventually, after what seemed like ages, I was able to stroke it and entice it out of the hedge. It let me take it by the collar and with some dexterity I led it back to my car.

By the time I got home, Sophie had gone to bed. Our dogs had started barking as I drove into the yard so she was awake.

'What's the time?' she asked blearily from under the duvet.

'It's a quarter to eleven,' I replied. 'I'm later than I intended because I found a dog by the road.'

She appeared from under the cover.

'You found a dog?'

'Yes, a little border terrier. Poor thing, it's very distressed.'

'Where is it? Have you brought it home?'

'Yes, it's in the kitchen by the Aga,' I told her. 'I've shut ours in the scullery.'

'Oh, I'm going to get up and see it,' she said, jumping out of bed with sudden alertness. Sophie adored dogs so this was quite an excitement.

The terrier, who I had already christened 'Foster', was drying by the Aga.

'Isn't he sweet,' Sophie exclaimed. 'Is it a he?'

'Yes,' I confirmed, adding, 'he's called Foster.'

She turned around. 'How do you know that?'

'Because that's the name I've just given him.'

'What a stupid name, why that?'

'Because Dr Foster went to Gloucester in a shower of rain, and I found him in the rain. And if we keep him, he would be fostered,' I explained, rather pleased with my reasoning.

'Are we going to keep him then?' she asked with delight.

'Well, we'll have to report him to the police. I mean, he looks well cared for and he's got a collar on so I suppose somebody's lost him.'

In fact, no one ever did claim the little old dog, which was rather sad. I guess that possibly his owners had tired of keeping an ageing pet and abandoned him on that horrible night. The vet thought he was about ten, and it shocked me to think that some heartless person could have just thrown out their pet after all those years. Inevitably, Foster remained with us as at Cordwainers, quickly, and with obvious delight, making friends with the other dogs.

Coincidentally, dogs were also on the agenda on my arrival at the office the following morning.

Gail was already in the office and in a considerable state of excitement. She was apt to get excited very easily, often over the most insignificant things. However, this morning's excitement was no small matter. The farm manager had rung in to say that there had been a disastrous case of sheep worrying, with twenty in-lamb ewes either killed or maimed by a pair of dogs.

I phoned him.

'Morning, Bill, I gather you've got a serious problem up there,' I said.

31

'Aye, we have, Mr Aden,' he replied. 'I expect Gail's told you about it but I've never seen such bloody carnage in my life before. Twenty ewes I've lost to these bloody dogs.'

He was clearly upset and angry.

'Have you seen the dogs?' I asked.

'Bloody right I have. They were at it when I went lookin' first thing this morning. There's a big German shepherd and some sort of collie cross thing.'

'Do you know whose they are?'

'Not yet, but we soon will. I've shot the soddin' German shepherd and the police have been up here. The collie got away but they reckon they'll find the owners of this other one.'

'Good, I'll come up and see you later, but in the meanwhile I'll see if we can find anything out about the dogs. I'm sure I've seen someone walking a German shepherd up near those new houses on the Glebe.'

'Well, anything you can do, Mr Aden, I'd appreciate. It makes my blood boil with rage to have this sort of thing happen. If folk can't keep control of their damned dogs they shouldn't have the bloody things. I just wish I'd shot the other bastard.'

As with all stockmen, Bill Bailey cared greatly for all the animals in his charge. The fact that they weren't pets and indeed, had a commercial use, made no difference. For some people it was incomprehensible that farmers, who raised animals to kill and eat, did care about them with passion during their often short lives.

'Gail,' I shouted across the hall, 'have you a

moment please.'

She came bustling across to my office, clad as always in tight revealing clothes which, to my mind, would have benefited from being less revealing.

I could never understand why some women elected to wear garments that were clearly too small for them. It was as though they had some mental urge to challenge every button and zip to the utmost.

She sat down opposite me and I fleetingly wondered what she would look like if all the buttons suddenly flew off. It wasn't an erotic thought, more one of a scientific study.

'You've heard about the sheep worrying up at the farm? Bill tells me he's shot a German shepherd, which I have a feeling lived up at the Glebe. I wonder if you know someone up there who might own it?'

Gail, in her enduring quest to find a suitable partner, made it her business to know almost everybody in the village.

'Well, I don't offhand,' she replied, 'but I can ask around if you like.'

'Please do. But don't let on what's happened. We want to find the owners before the news gets out. If we can't identify the owners we can't take any action, and my guess is that they'll disown it if they realise what's happened.'

'Okay,' she said, 'I'll be discreet.' And with a mission in hand she bustled out.

The other staff had arrived by then and I could hear her excitedly recounting the morning's drama. Discretion wasn't a word I would have used in connection with Gail.

By lunchtime she had the answer.

'That dog belongs to Mr and Mrs Cronk,' she told me. 'They live at a house called "Chez Nous", which, as you guessed, is in the Glebe.'

At about the same time Bill Bailey rang.

'The police have had a worried call from the owners,' he explained. 'They've gone in to collect the dog, or what's left of it.'

'That's excellent, Bill,' I replied. 'Once the police have confirmed everything I'll contact the owners and let them know we intend to prosecute.'

I didn't particularly relish the task as, presumably, they would be distressed at losing their dog. Nonetheless it was their responsibility to keep the animal under control and frankly any dog owner has to accept that responsibility.

I imagined a bereaved couple, gently sobbing into white linen handkerchiefs, but this vision was rudely transformed mid-afternoon when a ferocious pair charged into the estate office. If owners are supposed to look like their pets, then these were the wrong people. I had a couple of human equivalents to pit bull terriers.

'Where's the f***ing bastard who shot my bloody dog?' I heard a man shout. 'I'll f***ing kill him.'

Fortunately all the staff were in, so we had numbers on our side.

Anne tried vainly to calm him down.

'You're the thieving bastard are you?' he shouted at me, jabbing a finger the size of a large pork sausage at me.

'No, I'm not,' I said, 'he doesn't work here and

would you be kind enough to stop shouting at us.'

He did stop, but unfortunately his wife started, and if anything her language was even worse.

'The f***ing police told us to come to the f***ing estate office as they were f***ing Sir Charles' f***ing sheep,' she yelled.

Clearly there was little likelihood of a reasonable conversation, or indeed an apology. I thought about suggesting that they apologised for letting their dog out to kill twenty sheep, but only fleetingly. Both Mr and Mrs Cronk, whom I presumed they were, not only had the character of gutter vocabulary, but the physical attributes that go with it.

They were both large to the extent of massive, but not fat, with a liking of tattoos and an abundance of ornate gold jewellery. The sheer volume of rings on their stubby fingers made me think of knuckle-dusters.

Having made their displeasure known, they stormed out, with threats of legal action hanging in the air.

In the end, of course, it was the estate that took legal action. The matter had to go to court, in view of the Cronks' absolute certainty that the estate was in the wrong for shooting their dog. Inevitably, the court found against them on every count.

Chapter 3

Two weeks before Christmas, Frampton held its annual fair and late night shopping event. It was always a jolly occasion and to me the start of Christmas proper.

The market square and the High Street were lined with stalls and most of the local shops stayed open until 8 pm.

The whole village took on a festive air and entered into the spirit of Christmas with much enthusiasm. The shop windows were gaily dressed and a plethora of coloured lights twinkled along the street and around the square. Many buildings had small Christmas trees mounted on brackets at the first floor level. The smell of roasting chestnuts, mulled wine and mince pies wafted in the air. It was a cold clear night with a magical and expectant atmosphere.

As agent to the estate it fell to me to act as chairman of the organising committee, which in effect meant delegating as much as possible to other people.

The most arduous task was undoubtedly dealing with the stallholders. The event had become well established locally and many traders attended year after year. The more commercial traders selling tacky soft toys or cheap brightly coloured pic'n'mix sweets took the event very seriously. For them it was a big business opportunity rather than simply a showcase or a chance to be part of the celebrations. Some of them were almost aggressive in their demands, even though they paid a peppercorn rent for their pitch.

It was perhaps an unfortunate mistake on my part therefore, to have delegated this part of the job to an extremely earnest young chap called Justin Fairweather. He had moved to the village six months earlier and was keen to engage in local activities.

I had noticed, during my time at Frampton, that local events tended to be run by two distinct types of character. There was the older fraternity, who sat on committees, partly because they had an interest in the activities and partly because they had sat on them for years. Inevitably those groups leant towards the more traditional type of village activity, such as bird watching, rambling and gardening. When it came to setting up a new committee for an innovative idea, such as the Christmas street fair, there was a general reluctance among the older members of the village to get involved.

This opened the door to the second category of people who enjoyed being involved in village life: the newcomers. There are always a number of folk who, as soon as they move to a new place, throw themselves in to community life with enormous energy and join just about every group that they can. Indeed those with special qualifications, such as an accountant, cause great excitement and are much sought after as treasurers on any number of committees.

By and large these willing individuals are welcomed by the community, with the odd exception of the occasional person who lets the power go to their head, and assumes an air of self-importance far greater than their role as chairman of the Ping-Pong Club.

Justin Fairweather wasn't the sort of man to become self-important. He seemed to have a genuine liking for the village, and a desire to make friends within it. At his first committee meeting he had appeared to be just the man for the job. Keen, organised, and with a fresh outlook, I had hoped that he would improve the variety of stalls, was meticulous and it appeared that anything anyone said was noted down in a little blue notebook, and his quick grasp of the organisational logistics was exceptional. Finally, I thought, we might upgrade the standard of stalls with his input. We wanted less of the fairground types and more selling local crafts and produce. Sir Charles had aptly summed up this situation the previous year, when he remarked, 'I don't think candy floss has much to do with a Suffolk Christmas. It's rather vulgar in my view.'

Initially, Justin Fairweather set about his task with great effect. He managed to persuade several local craft-type people to display their wares, together with a couple of local food producers. He increased the number of stalls, so that on the night both the High Street and the market square were lined stall to stall with an enticing variety of wares.

A research scientist, Justin was organised and efficient but somewhat shy. Very serious and apparently with no sense of humour, he was brilliant on paper but less so when dealing with people. For a start he wouldn't look you in the eye, he had a slightly effeminate manner and a most appalling handshake. It was akin to grabbing hold of a spaniel's ear after it had been swimming in a pond.

None of this put him in good stead when the stallholders began to arrive. Despite his meticulous planning, which included a scale drawing of the stalls' layout, some traders resented being moved from their positions of previous years. A lot of un-Christmas-like language followed, and a nervous Justin summoned me over for some support. Between us we placated them with tact and diplomacy, telling them: 'If you don't shut up then you won't come next year.'

It made me reflect on the way that so many people manage to stress themselves over relatively little matters. It didn't seem to me to be a matter of huge concern as to whether one's stall was directly outside the Anne of Cleves or six feet to one side even though such matters seemed to be keeping me in gainful employment. Nearly every day, and certainly every week, there was some trivial matter upon which I was obliged to adjudicate.

The latest had been a minor boundary dispute. Two cottage neighbours, one in an estate house, the other privately owned, had fallen out over which side of the dividing down pipe should the decorating stop. Most of the cottages fronting the streets in Frampton were lath and plaster with colour-washed walls and the variety of colours was a particular feature of the landscape in this part of Suffolk.

The private owner wanted to include the down pipe and our tenant thought otherwise. Frankly, from the estate's point of view I couldn't care less. In fact they could paint the whole wall and save us a job.

I had been called to attend a meeting of the warring factions.

The estate's tenant, to give him some credit, was only as he put it, protecting our interests.

'Mr Aden,' started Hugh Postlethwaite, 'I'm so grateful you've come up. I'm afraid there's bad news.'

'And what is that?' I asked.

'Mr Green has got paint on our down pipe,' he explained, pointing earnestly at a smudge of something up near the gutter.

'I've told you, Hugh,' Mr Green cut in, 'I haven't finished the job yet. I've to finish the line and then paint the pipe.'

'Ah, but that's just the point. You'll be on our side if you do that.'

'No, I won't,' Mr Green went on, 'my frontage is 15' 6" according to the plan in my deeds, and that's where 15' 6" comes.'

'Well, Mr Aden will know where we are with the estate's deeds then, won't you, Mr Aden?'

'I'm afraid I won't,' I explained, 'and with respect to your measurements, Mr Green, there is no way you can be accurate to six inches on a plan that has probably been several times copied, and will be at a relatively small scale.'

'No, you're wrong there, Mr Aden,' Mr Green said. 'I've rung the Ordnance Survey and they say all their plans are to scale.'

'Yes, they are,' I agreed, 'but the scale you have is ridiculous. It's far too small and in any case it's photocopied, which distorts it.'

There was a silence while Mr Green dwelt on his assumed six inches.

'I'm grateful to you, Mr Postlethwaite, for keeping an eye on the estate's interests, but provided the cottages look smart I'll be happy to let the painting finish, irrespective of the exact boundary.'

'Well I suppose so,' Hugh Postlethwaite muttered, 'but I don't want to be held responsible for the loss of Sir Charles' property.'

I thought that was rather exaggerating the point but nevertheless assured him that all would be well.

Mr Green was clearly delighted, although I made it abundantly clear that Mr Postlethwaite had been right to query the position. Nonetheless it made me wonder. Why on earth didn't they just agree something and be done with it? Why didn't people in general agree things and get on with it?

The sound of 'Jingle Bells' brought me back to the moment. Father Christmas was careering down the High Street on his sleigh. To be more accurate, Jack Howdego, who ran the village garage, was careering down the High Street on a contraption that had a remarkable resemblance to a ride-on lawnmower.

This happened every year. It was the highlight of Mr Howdego's calendar and possibly somebody else's as well. Still, it all helped provide the appropriate ambience, which was greatly enhanced by the Salvation Army band striking up in the square.

I hurried up Market Passage to see them. Although with each passing year the band dwindled, the remaining veterans could still produce the most wonderful sounds. People started to congregate around the Christmas tree in the centre of the square and join in the carols, bringing the traditional spirit of Christmas to the village festivities.

This was Sir Charles' big moment. It was the only part of the street fair he particularly liked, and he strode about handing out song sheets, encouraging everyone to join in. The more people that sang the better. Sir Charles was tone deaf, but what he lacked in tune he made up for in volume. The beginning of the carol singing was always a most awful noise that would set dogs off howling and children crying. But once enough voices joined in some kind of melodic tune evolved ... not quite the voice of angels, but on the way.

The Christmas fair was a good time in the village. By and large all differences were forgotten and people simply got on with having fun. The early part of the evening was for everyone – children, parents and grandparents – what with the stalls, the singing of a few carols, some rather primitive fairground rides and a generous amount of mulled wine.

I think it was due to a generous amount of mulled wine that Gail nearly didn't make it to Christmas. One or two folk referred to her as the village bicycle, which was a bit unfair, if only because she didn't have wheels. What she did have, however, was a thirst for male company and a pair of enormous breasts. Inevitably this combination often led to situations that escalated out of control, with the carnage of the aftermath brought into the estate office the next day.

By 9 pm, the fair was winding down and the pubs were starting to get going, Sir Charles had gone home and I called in at the Anne of Cleves for a pint before doing the same. As I entered, through a haze of cigarette smoke, I heard Gail call over.

'Hi, James,' she shouted. 'Come over and have one on me.'

I pushed my way through the crowd, half of whom I knew, to reach Gail's table.

'What'll you have?' she slurred, as the two men either side of her eyed me menacingly.

'A pint of Abbots, thank you,' I replied, not particularly wanting to join her table but too polite to walk away. She tottered off to the bar on some extremely high, possibly fashionable, certainly inappropriate, stilettos. The two men watched her carefully with no doubt a degree of lust, before returning their gaze to me.

I introduced myself, as I knew neither of them.

'Where are you from?' I enquired, in an effort to engage them in some sort of conversation.

They stared back as if I had asked them whether their parents had been married when they were born.

After several moments of silence, one said, 'Bury St Edmunds.'

'Oh, not far away then,' I commented, blundering valiantly on. 'Not a bad place to live.'

Another long pause developed and I glanced over towards the bar hoping to see Gail returning with my beer. To my dismay she was still waiting to be served.

'It's the bloody pits,' one of them muttered.

'Oh,' I replied, not knowing which one had spoken.

Briefly I thought of Christmas cheer and good-will to all men, before deciding that I was on a lost cause. So I sat there and waited for what seemed an extraordinarily long time for Gail to return.

'Sorry I was so long,' she said, 'but there was a huge queue.'

The two men brightened visibly on her return, although the conversation remained non-exist-ent. They seemed happy simply to stare at her breasts.

Courageously I remained chatting to Gail for a further five minutes but clearly the amount, or strength, of the mulled wine was considerable. As soon as it was relatively polite to do so I left to chat with some tenant farmers, leaving Gail to communicate somehow with her new admirers. It was clear that the communication was more physical than verbal, so it was no surprise to hear the next morning that shortly after closing time a fight had broken out between the two men. Gail's attributes, whilst plentiful, were obviously not enough to share.

Chapter 4

The following week an old friend of mine rang to invite me shooting up in Northumberland.

'A few locals have taken a day on a neighbouring farm,' he explained, 'and there's a spare gun.'

'Peter, that's very kind. I'd love to come up. What date is it?'

'Saturday the twentieth,' he replied. 'I'm afraid it's a bit short notice but it would be great to see you if you can make it.'

I had a look through my diary, which was free for that date.

'Come up on the Friday night and of course bring Sophie if she would like to come as well.'

The arrangements were duly confirmed, although Sophie had a friend's hen party in London that weekend, and clearly anticipated more excitement there than chasing pheasants out of the woods in Northumberland.

I particularly enjoyed shooting just before Christmas as everyone always appeared to be in a jovial and relaxed frame of mind.

We left Mrs Painter, our housekeeper, in charge of Emma and the house and set off on our respective journeys. It was a long drive from Suffolk to Berwick upon Tweed, in fact the best part of nearly six hours. The A1, or Great North Road as I preferred to call it, seemed an interminable ribbon of tarmac overly cluttered with vehicles. The view through the Midlands seemed drab but once past the collieries and power stations of Nottinghamshire and South Yorkshire, the countryside took on a more pleasant aspect as the traffic thinned.

I pulled into a service station somewhere north of Pontefract for a cup of tea and to refuel. I was abruptly reminded that there were two major problems with such service stations. Firstly, the food, secondly, the people. A pot of tea arrived containing brown water and the tea seemed as likely to have originated from India as the waiter.

I drove round on to the forecourt to fill up the car with diesel. I couldn't help noticing that the price indicator flicked around far faster than the litres of fuel going into the tank. I had contemplated travelling by train but with Bramble, my black Labrador, and a gun, I foresaw complications. Added to that was the fact that travelling from Bury St Edmunds to Berwick upon Tweed meant two changes of trains, with the result that the journey would have taken me most of the weekend. I could have travelled more efficiently to the Congo.

Back on the Great North Road, I felt refreshed by the brief break. Before long I had reached Scotch Corner, which was always a milestone on my journeys north. After that, the open countryside of County Durham and Northumberland beckoned, with only Newcastle to circumnavigate. Inevitably we ground to a halt near the Angel of the North statue, a quite striking modern sculpture that well deserves its accolades.

46

We gradually inched past the Metro Centre at Gateshead, before finding the road cleared as we headed north towards Alnwick.

Despite the many signs by the side of the road informing me that hundreds of people had been killed in the last three years on that particular section of road, I managed to reach Berwick unscathed, with not a corpse strewn over the bonnet of my car.

Peter and his family lived in a splendid Victorian pile on the edge of Berwick upon Tweed. I had known Peter since I shared lodgings with him at college and was godfather to his eldest son. I always enjoyed staying, with him and his wife Clarissa, as their hospitality was exceptional. Peter was one of the most frugal and careful of my friends, but Clarissa made up for it by being a superb cook.

I had taken the precaution of packing thermal underwear which meant that the freezing cold house would not prevent me from enjoying a delicious dinner and some good wine.

To be fair, Peter had lit a fire in the drawing room, which had a cheering effect. However, the efficiency of the fire in relation to the size of the room was similar to sitting by a candle in the Royal Albert Hall.

The next morning, Clarissa prepared a cooked breakfast to set us on our way. The shoot was being held on a small farm about ten miles away on some quite open hill country which had been sparsely planted with a few coverts.

I knew about half the people there and was introduced to the other guns. They seemed a

47

jovial lot, a good collection of random tweeds and gun dogs setting the scene for a day's sport. Peter had organised some hot soup for our arrival, which was devoured eagerly by the guests.

It was a beautiful day, sunny, clear but with a fairly ferocious wind blowing in off the sea. I wondered how the birds would fly.

The first drive went well. The beaters pushed steadily through the wood, sending a sparse but regular number of pheasants over the guns, the birds soon climbing high, making for some testing and enjoyable shooting. However, the second and third drives were not so impressive. Whilst the birds were there, they tended to fly low out of the coverts providing poor, if any, sport.

We then stopped for a break whilst the beaters went on to a distant wood. Some welcome hot coffee was provided, together with the additional comfort of a tot of sloe gin.

Peter explained that this syndicate shoot was a new venture and that it was their first year. They had been experimenting as to which way to drive the woods and where to position the guns. The shoot captain who organised the days was enthusiastic although inexperienced.

Peter told me, 'We have tried beating through this wood in the other direction, but all the birds simply turned and flew back into the wood, so this time we shall be standing the guns at the opposite end.'

In due course we made our way to our next pegs, or at least vague positions where we should stand, and waited.

We could hear the beaters in the distance,

tapping their sticks and yelling, 'Get up, get up.' Not much appeared for some time. Occasionally a bird would fly over, giving everyone a bit of a jump, but it wasn't until the beaters were nearly at us that the birds began to fly.

Disappointingly they flew low, as if they knew that by doing so they would remain safe. With some dismay, I noticed that the gun to my left had taken several shots at rather low birds. Peter, who was standing on his left, was gesticulating that the man should keep his gun higher. The gun either did not comprehend, or was too intent on bagging his numbers, when I heard a shot and felt a sudden, severe, stinging sensation in my head.

Almost immediately blood began to pour from my nose, and I realised what had happened. I broke my gun and shouted across to the gun on my right.

'I've been shot.'

'You've what?' he shouted back.

'I've been shot,' I repeated, this time loudly enough for the guns on either side to have heard me clearly.

I was in a state of shock, and although not in any great pain, I was alarmed by the amount of blood pouring from my head. By this time the message had got around the rest of the guns who started running towards me.

The injury could only have been caused by one person, and that was the gun standing slightly behind me and to the left. It transpired later on that he was a most inexperienced shot, and that this was one of his first outings on a driven game shoot.

Understandably he was upset by what had happened. Not nearly as upset as I was though. There was a good deal of fussing around whilst everyone offered their thoughts on what to do next. I half thought that we should simply carry on, but the bleeding hadn't lessened, which worried me.

The person who shot me was a dentist. I had always been scared of dentists since I was a small boy. Clearly well justified.

They decided that I should go to hospital and the dentist offered to drive me there in his car. I sat down on the verge by a gateway, trying in vain to stop the flow of blood. Everyone else clucked around like a flock of hens, not sure what to do or say. Within a few moments a shiny new black Range Rover appeared (he was in private practice), and I was whisked at speed to a small hospital in Berwick upon Tweed.

It was immediately evident that the cottage hospital in Berwick was not used to shooting incidents. Worse still, being a Saturday lunchtime, there were hardly any staff and although the nurses were helpful they were unable to offer much advice. Eventually they summoned a locum doctor and he too appeared helpful, though unwilling to take charge of the situation. His command of English medical terms seemed limited. In fact his command of English was limited. I did not feel entirely comfortable with the situation and nor did the nurses.

They suggested that I should go to a much bigger hospital, either in Edinburgh or Newcastle upon Tyne, both of which were sixty miles distant. I decided upon Newcastle and the head nurse helpfully phoned ahead to warn them of my arrival. The dentist drove with a sense of urgency, I suspect not least because he did not want to incur many more bloodstains on his upholstery. However, he was clearly concerned about my wellbeing and embarrassed at being in such a position.

It was late afternoon by the time we reached Newcastle hospital. Our entrance in the A&E department caused a stir, not so much because of the blood on my head, that was sort of expected in a hospital, but rather because I was still wearing my tweed plus fours and Wellington boots. The nurse on the reception desk, having been warned of my arrival, was quick to show me into a consulting room and the doctor on duty arrived within a few minutes. It seemed that they were used to shooting incidents in Newcastle upon Tyne on a Saturday.

Despite that, the doctor, who must have been a junior, was not quite sure what to do. I went off for numerous X-rays, which showed four lead pellets lodged at various places in my head. When I returned to the consulting room a more senior house doctor had arrived. The two discussed the X-rays and were concerned that two pieces of shot in particular were rather close to vital parts.

In the end they decided, after referring the matter to a consultant, that they could do nothing for me that night but that it was safe for me to return to Berwick.

I left all my details with them, including my mobile phone number, and they made me promise that I would arrange to see the consultant in

51

Bury St Edmunds on Monday when I returned home.

The dentist and I set off back to Berwick but we had only travelled for about ten minutes when my mobile phone rang. It was the consultant, asking me to return to the hospital urgently. This put me in a terrible panic as I imagined they had since found something far more sinister.

I was ushered back through the A&E waiting room, once again the object of curious stares, to see the consultant. Much to my relief he assured me that they had not found anything further but, on reflection, they felt I ought to spend the night in hospital under close observation.

It was a relief, but not much of one. If there is anything I dislike more than dentists it is hospitals, and the thought of spending Saturday night there was most unappealing. I discussed it with the doctors but my fear of something dreadful happening during the night as I lay in my bed in Berwick was worse than my fear of staying in hospital. In Berwick I would be sixty miles from a decent hospital and in an emergency would only be able to count on a doctor who couldn't speak English.

The dentist, who I could sense was becoming tired by all this drama, departed for the dinner party that Peter and his wife were holding that evening. The doctors had assured me that if I wanted to venture into Newcastle for an hour or two then they could see no reason why that should be a problem. I, however, did see why it would be a problem, I had blood in my hair and on my face, and I was wearing tweed plus fours and Wellington boots. Newcastle upon Tyne may have a reputation for a lively nightlife but I had an inkling that I would draw unwelcome attention to myself. Besides which I had just been shot in the head and did not really feel like a night out on the town.

Fortunately I had my wallet with me and I wandered to a local shop where I bought a magazine and something basic to eat. A bed had been made ready for me in one of the wards and I was instructed to return by 8 pm.

By the time I got to the ward a rumour had spread, throughout both the staff and patients, that a man had been shot. Perhaps it wasn't quite such a common occurrence in Newcastle after all, as people eyed me up as I walked past.

The very kind nurses made me as comfortable as they could in the circumstances, but I had nothing to change into and nothing much to do apart from read my magazine.

The other patients around me were either overly talkative or dying, which didn't bode well for an evening of scintillating conversation. As soon as I could I climbed into the bed and pretended to sleep. It was a most dreadful night with constant comings and goings by hospital staff and ominous noises coming from some of the other patients.

The night passed and I was discharged by the doctor by mid-morning the next day. Peter had kindly brought my car down to Newcastle and, although feeling a little jaded, I felt well enough to drive home. The whole appalling experience had made me feel both nervous and contemplative.

There were a lot of 'what ifs' going through my mind. An inch to the side would have caught me in the eye.

The consultant at Bury St Edmunds felt it would do more harm than good to remove any of the shot so, for the time being, the matter was laid to rest.

Since then I have been through metal detectors at airport security and not set off the alarm. And the fact that I have had a filling, carried out by a private dentist at no cost, is some consolation.

Chapter 5

Sir Charles was very keen on his shooting and his woodland. He had been dismayed to hear about my accident in Northumberland.

'A chap like that should never be allowed on the shooting field!' he exclaimed. 'It's the absolute duty of every host to make sure their invited guns are safe, know the etiquette. Had this chap got no idea?'

'At the moment, Sir Charles, I'm not sure of all the details,' I explained, 'but I'm sure in time I'll find out.'

'Well, he should never go out again to my mind,' he said. 'Apart from the danger, it brings the sport into disrepute. It's bad enough with these inexperienced guns wounding birds, rather than killing them cleanly, without them shooting the person next to them.'

In an effort at joviality, I replied, 'Well I'm rather pleased he wounded me, rather than killed me outright.'

The discussion then moved on from shooting to woods in general. Sir Charles' estate included nearly 1,000 acres of woodland managed carefully for timber production, amenity and conservation values. The conservation value of his woodlands included their use for sport.

Currently, Sir Charles had something else on his mind to do with woodlands and had become quite passionate about the idea.

'I was with a friend of mine, in fact you know him – your old boss Lord Leghorn, who told me he has planted what he calls a community woodland for his village.'

'Oh, has he?' I asked. 'I wonder where they've planted that – I can't recall him particularly wanting to do anything like that when I was there.'

'Well he has, I'm not sure where it is but I gather it's a little spinney somewhere near the estate village, which has been planted for the benefit of the community.'

'Yes, I've heard about such ideas,' I replied, 'it's all to do with this business of trying to engage local people in taking an interest in the surrounding countryside.'

'Yes,' continued Sir Charles, 'I think it's a marvellous idea. What I'd like to do is to find maybe a couple of acres of land near the village, organise some planting, which eventually will form a little woodland to which anyone can have access. You know, for walking the dog or having a picnic, that sort of thing.'

It didn't seem such a bad idea and indeed with Sir Charles' philanthropic views, particularly towards his social responsibilities towards the village, it was surprising that perhaps he hadn't suggested it before.

He went on, 'I've been doing a bit of research and it seems to be quite the done thing nowadays. Most of it is led by councils and fund-raising type things, but I don't see why, if I provide the land, we shouldn't get on and do the thing here.'

I agreed and added, 'I'll have a think and perhaps suggest two or three locations for you to consider.'

'Excellent,' said Sir Charles, 'and what I think you should do is go and visit one of these so-called community forests to see what they do. We can learn from that and put it into practice.'

I had read articles about community forests, which were now springing up all over the country. They were mainly in deprived areas, or regeneration areas as the government preferred to call them, and generally funded by the State. However, Sir Charles was right, it would be useful to see how they went about these things and use some of the ideas on the estate.

A couple of weeks later, in late January, I arranged to visit the National Forest in the Midlands. I travelled over to the borders of Leicestershire and Staffordshire to meet their programme manager, John Wire. He explained that he had had training in forestry but was more inclined towards woodland use for people, rather than simply timber, which was how he had got his present job. He did strike me more as a social worker than a forester but he was certainly knowledgeable on all aspects of planting a community woodland.

We spent an hour or so in his office, looking at their ambitious plans to plant thousands of acres of woodland across the Midlands, and the details of how to engage the local communities. It was all much more complicated and ambitious than Sir Charles' two-acre wood, but there were some useful points that we could use.

A lot of the National Forest schemes had to

meet government objectives and of course these included an element of political correctness. At Frampton we could be sure there would be none of that. Mr Wire's suggestion that we should involve ethnic minorities would have no relevance in Frampton as the nearest we got to an ethnic minority was a Sumatra bantam owned by Hugh Postlethwaite.

Nonetheless there were plenty of other good reasons why we should have a community woodland and I set off with Mr Wire on a short trip through the forest.

The National Forest seemed to be no more than a random scattering of twigs across a dreary landscape. I didn't of course mention that to Mr Wire, and I am sure that in 100 years it will look quite different. Indeed without the vision and forward planning of landowners and farmers much of the British landscape would look very different today. The twenty-first century's landscape architects from such organisations as the National Forest would enhance that vision.

I was struck by the different motivations for past and present landscape design. The aristocracy, such as Sir Charles, who had owned great swathes of countryside for hundreds of years, generally planted woods or created lakes or parks for their own enjoyment. Whether that be sporting, financial or simply amenity reasons made little difference. In essence they did it for themselves, and because they could. Fortunately their great work was, and still is, a benefit to the rest of the population.

Newer plantings were by and large created by

government or quango. The only factor that was the same between the two was the amenity value, particularly in terms of access and landscape. Community forests, or woodlands, had no commercial value really and were quite possibly the reverse, in that they needed huge amounts of public money to set them up. As for sport, that was definitely not in the minds of the planners. Cycling and walking were the highest priorities.

Although I wouldn't describe these new woodlands as municipal parks, there were certain similarities between the two. Instead of muddy paths and old wooden stiles, these places had carefully made stone tracks and tidy little gates to allow wheelchair access. They weren't really the type of woodlands that I would choose to walk in but upon reflection, as I was driving home, I realised that effectively the public were paying for these woods so they should be designed for the greater public's benefit.

Sir Charles was interested in my report on the visit but I could sense that he was not overly excited about the prospect of an all-access disability trail, or becoming restricted by some grant-awarding institution.

'No, no,' he said, 'we'll do this my way. If I'm giving the land to the village and paying for the trees then I'll decide what it looks like.'

'I'm sure that's a good idea, Sir Charles,' I replied, 'but in order to get some proper community spirit we need to get the village involved with the planting and to take some responsibility for its well-being.'

I proposed several little pieces of land adjoining

the village, where with my agent's hat on I was certain had no development potential. Sir Charles chose an area in the corner of Church Field, and plans were duly put forward to the parish council.

The council were very enthusiastic about the idea and inevitably set up a sub committee and posted an announcement in the *Parish News*, asking for volunteers to join it.

The sub committee was chaired by one of the parish councillors, Philip Gadsby, an eminently sensible and pragmatic chap, held in my esteem not least because he was a retired land agent. He gathered together some worthies who felt they had an affinity for trees, and the project got under way. I had been asked to sit on the committee as Sir Charles' representative, which I was pleased to do. It was all very well Sir Charles donating two acres of land to the village, but it was also important that the project evolved in what he would consider an appropriate manner.

Philip Gadsby took charge admirably. He delegated the community involvement and fundraising to others, but more or less kept the planting design to himself with my input. The fundraising part was relatively simple as Sir Charles was giving the land and trees. Some gates, a noticeboard and a couple of benches were the only extras.

The community involvement part was more complicated. The idea was that if people could be persuaded to help plant the trees then they would take an interest in the area as it evolved. But getting community involvement is not an easy task, and certainly one that requires patience. My own view that a benign dictatorship is a far better way to achieve results would not have been appropriate in this situation. I kept well out of it.

I did notice a flurry of correspondence exchanged via the parish newsletter, some of which was helpful, some not. One particular resident who I didn't know suggested that there should be a tarmac path through the middle with street lights so that it could be used during the evenings.

The response that she should move back to Chingford, or wherever it was that she came from, seemed to be supported by most of the village, but the lady herself took great offence.

Under Philip Gadsby's direction a sensible plan was formed which seemed to encompass most villagers' views and was acceptable to Sir Charles. In due course we fenced off the area and set it aside for planting in early March.

Sir Charles' son and heir, Sebastian, had moved to the village about a year previously with his new wife Serena. They were living in a large old house called Bulls Place Farmhouse. Sebastian was a professor of anthropology at Cambridge and although he had a great liking for the estate, he had very little worldly knowledge. He was Sir Charles's only close relative, his wife having died years before and they had no other offspring. He was keen that Sebastian should integrate and become involved with estate affairs as in due course he would inherit the lot.

It was decided that Sebastian should be there on the day to commemorate the first planting in the new woodland, particularly as this exercise was a step into the twenty-first century. It seemed appropriate that he, who would presumably own and lead the estate through the next fifty years, should be seen clearly as the heir apparent.

Sebastian had no practical idea of estate matters and this was of great concern to his father. For my part I hoped that Sir Charles would live to a great age, giving Sebastian a chance to grow into the role.

It occurred to me just how unworldly he was when I visited him to discuss this opening ceremony and we sat in his freezing cold study in semi darkness.

It was 3.30 pm on a January day so the light was fading outside. He had a couple of candles flickering on his desk and it rather fitted with the abstemious eccentricities that he had clearly inherited from his father.

However, he surprised me by saying, 'This damn power cut's been two days now, I would have thought the electric people would have sorted it out ages ago.'

'Power cut?' I enquired.

'Yes,' he said, 'we've been without electricity for about a day and a half in fact. Haven't you got the same problem up in the village?'

'No,' I replied, 'I don't think we've had any power cut, let alone for a day and a half. Are you sure there's not something wrong in this house?'

'Well I didn't think so,' he said. 'I just assumed that all the power was off. I hadn't really thought to see if anyone else was off.'

'Have you rung the electricity people,' I enquired, 'they would know if the power was off for a reason.'

'Erm, no, I expect a lot of people will have done that already.'

Personally I doubted whether anyone would have rung as the sole victim in this power cut seemed to be Sebastian's house.

'I'll go and have a look at the switchboard and see what might have happened there,' I suggested.

I borrowed one of his candles and walked slowly along the passageway to the scullery where the main fuseboard was located. It only took me a minute to realise what had happened. There was a shelf of books above the main trip switch and clearly one had fallen off, hitting the switch on the way down, cutting off the electricity supply. So, with a simple flick power was restored.

Clearly if this was the shape of things to come when he moved into the Hall then he was going to need a huge retinue of staff to keep the show on the road.

The following day, Sir Charles called in to see me at the estate office to discuss a concern he had with Sebastian, or more particularly about Serena. He was so beside himself with anguish that he failed to notice the resplendent redecoration of the estate office and didn't even question whether the lavatories had been painted in estate green.

'Come and sit down in my office, Sir Charles,' I offered, 'you look quite distraught.'

He bustled into my room but was quite incapable of sitting in a chair. He paced up and down in front of my desk.

'I am absolutely appalled,' he went on. 'I think Sebastian should have dealt with this before it got out of hand. Serena has quite overstepped the mark and it is not the sort of thing that we can afford to do in this family.'

I had no idea what he was talking about and I doubted that it could have much significance, having seen Sebastian the day before when there had been no mention of any excitements from him.

'I just can't believe it. I just can't understand the mentality of some people.' He continued, 'You know we've had hundreds of years of practice in keeping this place together, being careful, good management and a certain amount of thriftiness.' This was a huge understatement. Sir Charles' idea of thriftiness was what most normal people would call meanness.

He insisted, for instance, that the central heating only operated during December and January and the rest of the time they relied on log fires with fuel provided by the estate. He only had two telephones in the house. At one point he instructed Hole that there should only ever be two light bulbs burning in the house during the evenings. One for Sir Charles and one for Hole. This particular instruction had led to both of them creeping about the house at night with torches and Hole falling over one of Sir Charles' poodles in the passageway. That particular money-saving idea was soon abandoned, but his view over motor cars remained firm.

This is what had caused his present anguish.

Sir Charles' only personal vehicle was a Morris

64

Traveller, which he deemed perfectly suitable for his use, both on the estate when it was fitted with snow chains so he could progress along muddy tracks, and, without chains generally on the roads in Suffolk. Outside Suffolk he travelled by train.

Sebastian had inherited his father's sense of thriftiness in this respect and drove a Reliant Robin, which, before he was married, had the passenger seat removed in order to accommodate his Irish Wolfhound, Argonaut. Since getting married though he had taken quite a rational view that it would be perfectly reasonable for Serena to be in the car with him and the dog, and they had bought an Audi estate car.

Sir Charles continued, 'Serena has bought another car and I can't understand why. They've already got two cars, why on earth would they want another one?'

On quiet reflection I thought that another car would be sensible. Sebastian's Reliant Robin, though still in active service, was generally confined to short trips around the estate. The Audi was their only proper car and relatively modest. Even that they had bought second-hand.

'She has bought,' he shouted, 'a bloody Range Rover!'

He grabbed the back of the chair and leant over it, gasping with incredulity. In fact I think he was shaking with rage. His long skinny hands, tainted with liver spots, gripped the back of the chair, the veins quite protruded.

I did not say anything for a while. I could see why Sir Charles was so distressed because I knew his nature. However, in the scheme of things to

65

come, Sebastian would shortly inherit not only the Frampton Hall Estate but land in Canada, Scotland and London, not to mention a huge portfolio of shares and one of the finest private art collections in Europe. So buying a new car, albeit an expensive one, was not going to plunge them into the never-never.

'A bloody Range Rover,' he said, 'a bloody Range Rover. They're the sort of thing that those drug dealers in the East End of London drive. It's black as well, with tinted windows. I mean, can you imagine the hideous thing? She's going to drive round Frampton in it and what on earth will everyone think? I mean, she's a lovely girl and all that but with those tinted windows people will be bound to think there's drugs involved.'

This was not going well. Clearly apart from the expense of the new car he was also worried about the image. This was surprising in a way as he never considered his own image, always wearing the same clothes whether he was at the Hall, in Frampton, or off to London on the train.

'Sir Charles,' I offered, 'I really don't think people will assume that sort of thing. Serena is very well liked as you know in the village and it is quite normal nowadays for farmers and land-owners to drive those cars. In fact they are very useful vehicles. They are good across country on these tracks here and also on the motorway if you're going to London or wherever.'

He continued gripping the back of the chair and didn't say anything, but the quivering began to subside. Suddenly he stood upright and shouted, 'And the cost. How on earth do they think they can afford such a car. It's a blatant extravagance, typical of the younger generation. If they start spending money like this the estate will be gone in a decade.'

It was at times like this that I realised my formal training in rural estate management at the Royal Agricultural College hadn't taught me what I needed to learn. So much of the running of an estate for a landowner relied on the skills of diplomacy, tact and comprehending the eccentric. It was all very well referring to the land agents' bible, *Walmsley's Estate Management,* but sometimes only experience helped.

'Sir Charles, I am sure that Sebastian and Serena will have considered all the costs of this car, and although I know it wouldn't be the sort of thing you would buy, I think it would be wise to let them create a new mould on the estate. After all, it is your wish that they become more involved and ready to take your place, and it is quite likely that their patronage will be different to yours. In most ways they have taken the same views that you have so perhaps the exception of a new car is something that must be accepted.'

Sir Charles by now had sat down in a chair and his distress abated somewhat. I felt a little sorry for him, now an elderly man really living in the past. His stature was still one of presence, tall, thin with a fine-shaped head and wispy white hair. He commanded his empire with almost puritanical concern, not only for the estate's survival but also for that of his tenants. This moment was a significant one in the sense of the change in the generations. Although Sir Charles would be, hopefully, alive for many years, the influence of the next generation would start to be felt.

It was only after Sir Charles left, somewhat placated, that I reflected on Sebastian's £50,000 Range Rover being considered an extravagance. The painting above the fireplace in Sir Charles' study was a Canaletto on which I had recently received an updated insurance valuation approaching £2 million. It was clear which would be the better investment but it wasn't possible to go shopping in a Canaletto.'

Chapter 6

Sophie and I lived about five miles from Frampton, just far enough for me to feel away from the estate and all its problems when I was at home.

Predominantly it was a sheep farm and Sophie managed it, with a bit of help from myself and a couple of farm workers, the elderly Flatt brothers. Since the arrival of Emma, however, Sophie had found it more difficult to do much hands-on work as she was preoccupied with the baby.

The sheep flock was divided into two. A third of the flock lambed early in January so that the lambs would be ready for the Easter market, and the remainder lambed at the traditional time of late March. As Sophie now had to take something of a back seat we had decided to employ a student to help at lambing time.

So far things seemed to be going well with a 180% lambing ratio and the student coping well with the farm workers. I would go and have a wander round the sheep after work and do what little bits and pieces I could to assist.

The student was a mid-year Harper Adams college chap called Dan. He was very capable, enthusiastic and managed to get on with the Flatts, which was no small feat. The two brothers, who lived in a pair of semi-detached cottages on the farm, rarely spoke to anyone, let alone each other. Somehow they managed to conduct their affairs through a series of grunts, nods and a sign language that appeared to rely on the manipulation of their flat caps. Dan, on the other hand, was very lively, talkative and articulate.

In fact it worked so well that my evening stints after work tended to be of little consequence, but I kept things tidy, which I at least thought important. I always maintained that just because farming could be a messy business, and lambing particularly so, it didn't mean the place had to look like a tip. I have a particular dislike of string, or more precisely baler twine. It has its uses, indeed important ones, and is tremendously useful for holding things together in an emergency. But I think it is an affront to any pastoral scene to see pieces of orange string tying up gates, doors, lying on the ground or, worst of all, holding up someone's trousers. Both the Flatt brothers preferred to used baler twine for this purpose despite my offer to buy them belts.

The sheep that we kept were Mules, bred in the Yorkshire Dales from a Wensleydale ewe crossed with a blue-faced Leicester ram. We then crossed the resultant ewes with a Suffolk ram, which produced a good commercial animal for the meat trade.

The January lambing always took place inside a large open-span building which could hold all the sheep. Along one side of the barn we erected temporary pens so that as each ewe lambed she could be taken into an individual pen with her new lambs, and carefully looked after for the first day or two. After that mother and babies would be turned out in a field close to the house.

'I said, ever since I had to get rid of a bag of prawns there's been a bit of trouble.'

'A bag of prawns!'

'Yes,' she said. 'I had a bag of prawns that went orf, and I didn't want them in the bin or they would stink all week, so I thought I'd flush them down the loo.'

'You flushed a bag of prawns down the loo,' I exclaimed, 'and you expect the estate to sort out the problem?'

'Well I read in some magazine,' she went on, 'that fish goes off in the bin so quick that it's best to flush it down the loo and then it's in the system.'

'And what system do you think that is?'

'Well you know, the system, the sewage works system and that.'

This was unusual even for Frampton.

'I don't suppose by any chance you emptied the bag before flushing it down?'

'Oh, no, no, no,' she said, 'that would let the smell out.'

'So you flushed a bag of prawns, in their polythene bag, down the loo?'

'Well, that's what it said to do in the magazine so that's what I did. I'm really sorry, Mr Aden, I didn't want to be any problem.'

'Well I have to say, Mrs Wilson, you are a problem and this is most irritating. Clearly, you have bunged up the sewer pipe with a polythene bag full of rotten prawns. Now you know that we always try to sort these matters out but in this case I think what you've done is unacceptable. You will have to arrange for the plumber to come and sort it out yourself, because I do not think this is the estate's responsibility.'

Mrs Wilson looked a little shocked, not only because she would have to organise the unblocking herself, but also because I had taken a rather dim view of the situation. Most of the tenants relied on the goodwill and co-operation of the estate to sort out many of their problems, but inevitably there were limits.

Unfortunately the episode didn't end quite there. Mrs Wilson, in an effort to avoid herself unnecessary expense, managed to get her prawns into the communal sewer behind the cottages. Although that solved her immediate problem it meant that two days later I was back on the scene because all the cottages further upstream, as it were, started to develop problems. With a communal problem it was far more difficult for the agent to walk away and I was called back again. My job was to try to identify the problem, rather than solve it, and I was certainly not in the habit of getting down on my knees and rodding drains.

After Anne had taken numerous calls I visited Mrs Wilson again.

'Did you get the plumber to come and sort out the problem,' I asked her.

'Well no, I didn't need to in the end, Mr Aden,' she explained. 'I just kept flushing and everything seemed to sort itself out so, if you'll excuse the pun, I think the problem just simply swum away.'

'Well I'm afraid it hasn't just swum away, Mrs Wilson, because we now have three cottages with a problem. I think all you've done is push it further down and blocked everyone else's drains.'

She raised a withered, frail hand to her lips. 'Ooh, I'm sorry, Mr Aden, I didn't mean to cause you any more trouble but I thought I'd solved it.'

I was becoming increasingly annoyed with Mrs Wilson.

'This is a matter that you should have dealt with, and now you've caused a problem for all your neighbours.'

I think she looked quite tearful but my resolve was hard.

'I will now deal with this situation, but – if I find the problem is with your prawns, then you will have to pay the bill.'

'Well I am sorry, Mr Aden, I really am, but I've only got my pension and that doesn't go far. I really think now it's out of my cottage, it's more of an estate matter.'

'Estate matter!' I bridled. 'I don't think it's an estate thing at all, Mrs Wilson. This is a problem that you have caused and you will have to deal with the consequences. I'm sorry that you only have your pension but frankly if anybody is going to stuff a bag of prawns down their lavatory, then they are asking for trouble.'

She looked a little frightened, and possibly distraught.

'You may only have a pension, Mrs Wilson,' I said, 'but do you really think its fair for the estate to foot the bill on this one?'

The plumber confirmed later that day that amongst all the other unmentionables he found in the sewer there was quite clearly a bag of prawns holding its own.

Chapter 7

The phone rang on my desk. 'I've got Mr Hole on the line for you,' announced Anne.

'Thank you, Anne, put him through.'

'Hello, James Aden here.'

'Hole here, Mr Aden, I've got Sir Charles on the line for you,' he announced.

Oh, dear, it was as I had feared. Sir Charles had instigated his alternative method of contacting people by telephone. I could vividly imagine the scenario that was about to unfold. Hole would have put his telephone receiver down on his desk in the butler's pantry and then proceeded, with no great urgency, along the passageways to Sir Charles' study. There he would inform Sir Charles that Mr Aden was on the telephone for him as requested.

Finally, Sir Charles picked up his handset. He then waited, audibly breathing into the mouthpiece, waiting for Hole to wind his way back to the butler's pantry and reset his phone before speaking. For most people this system would be ridiculous but not, of course, of course, at Frampton Hall.

'Is that James? Sir Charles speaking here from the Hall,' he declared.

'Good morning, Sir Charles,' I replied warmly.

'Ah, good,' he said, 'Hole has just put me through. No, Hole has just put you through I think,' he said.

'Yes, Sir Charles, we are now in communication.'

'Indeed we are,' he replied, 'indeed. Now I asked Hole to get you on the line because I've got something to say to you.'

There was a shuffling of papers and hesitation. He had clearly forgotten why he was ringing me, which was not altogether surprising considering the time lag between his initial thought and eventually getting me on the telephone.

'Are you still there, Sir Charles?' I asked.

'Yes, yes, yes I am but I'm just looking at these papers and, erm, I'm trying to remember what it was that I needed to discuss. Erm, erm...' and in the background I heard, 'Do get off, Monty, you damn thing.' He was talking to one of his standard poodles with him in the study.

'Ah, yes, Monty's just reminded me. I was out walking this morning and I've come across a rather exciting find. I wondered if I could show you.'

'By all means, Sir Charles, what have you found?'

'I'd rather not say over the public telephone system,' he said, 'but if you can come up here tomorrow morning early, we'll take the same route that I walked this morning and I can show you. It might be of great importance.'

'Can you tell me where you've made this exciting discovery?'

'I'm really not able to over the public telephone, James, but I have marked my find with a stick so I can take you to exactly the right place tomorrow.'

I was surprised that, if it was so exciting, he did not want to rush out straightaway and despite my misgivings as to how exciting it would be, I was eager to discover the cause of his enthusiasm.

'I would go today, James, but I'm about to go orf to London for a new pair of shoes and it'll be dark by the time I get back.'

'Very well, Sir Charles, let us hope that whatever you've found will stay there until tomorrow.'

'Oh, it'll stay there all right. I have a feeling it's been there for quite some time.'

This was even more intriguing. Perhaps he had discovered the ruins of an ancient building. Or at least that was all I could think of at the time, save for something that some walker had dropped and alerted Sir Charles' interest. Anyway, I would have to wait.

I had a full and busy day in the office catching up on the mundane paperwork which was the bane of any agent's life. Apart from the what I called 'people' things, which referred to dealing with tenants and so on, there was a seemingly never-ending load of papers to go through. Over the years the bureaucrats have seen fit to burden us with forms for this and forms for that, supposedly in order to made our lives much safer, healthier and happier. Of course, whether these changes have been for the good is open to debate.

I had, for instance, in front of me on my desk a request from one of our tenants to confirm that firstly, she was a tenant and secondly, that she had always paid her rent. The tenant was trying to open a new bank account and deposit £200. From what I could make out of the accompanying literature from the bank, they and the government were concerned that my tenant was a money-laundering expert, filtering funds to a terrorist group in the Middle East.

I had never thought that Mrs Benbrow, a seventy-five-year-old widow, whose husband had worked as a footman in the Hall for over fifty years, was likely to engage in such activities. I suppose appearances can be deceptive but when she arrived later in the day, struggling into the estate office on two walking sticks, money laundering and terrorism didn't spring to mind.

Aside from my gallant assistance in helping our country avert the threat of another terrorist coup, I had plenty more letters to dictate, cheques to sign, and minor decisions to make.

When the office closed at 5 pm I had had quite enough. I tried to mix my days with meetings, visits out on to the estate and office work, and therefore avoid long days behind my desk. It wasn't always possible.

I had promised Sophie that I would collect some fish and chips from Bury St Edmunds on the way home, as she had had rather a busy day on the farm as Dan had finished and returned home at the weekend.

It was a slight detour to go from Frampton to Bury St Edmunds and then back home to Cordwainers but well worth it. Not only did it mean no one had to cook or wash up as we ate the meal out of the paper, but the fish and chip shop was an excellent one. Why they called it The Codpiece I was never quite sure.

My usual route home was blocked by an accident at Sicklesmere on the main road so I had to divert along the back lanes. Even though it was dark the charm of the lime-washed coloured cottages so typical of Suffolk was a delight. Most of the villages had a green, or tye, a pretty stone flint church and a cluster of multicoloured houses surrounding it. I dwelt on the fact that with our busy life at Cordwainers with the farm, and my immersion in estate affairs at Frampton, Sophie and I had little time to explore the immediate neighbourhood. I resolved that we should make more time to spend with each other and with Emma, discovering the local countryside.

When I got home, Sophie was in the drawing room holding Emma on her lap, having lit the fire in the inglenook. It was a heart-warming and beautiful sight to see my stunning wife and our daughter waiting for me.

Sophie managed to eat her supper using one hand and a fork whilst cradling Emma in her other arm. I meanwhile devoured mine quickly, having not eaten much all day. When I finished I took Emma and held her for a while, letting Sophie finish her meal. She then took the baby up to her bed.

This was the time of the evening that I really enjoyed. The fire was burning brightly, throwing out enormous amounts of heat into our cosy sitting room. The large comfortable sofas were designed to envelop and almost caress you. I took a moment to reflect on the style with which Sophie had designed the interior of our house. When we had inherited it from her uncle the place was quite grand but somewhat austere and formal. As a bachelor there had been no feminine touches and one had always felt slightly uncomfortable when visiting Cordwainers Hall. Sophie had changed all that and the soft pale green carpets, floor-length curtains and comfortable chairs and sofas had made it welcoming. We still had her uncle's frighteningly valuable paintings on the walls and some beautiful antique furniture dotted around the room, but you did now feel that you could kick off your shoes, sprawl on the sofa and relax.

Sometimes we watched television but that night we sat and talked. I explained that Sir Charles had found some exciting discovery that he was going to show me the following morning.

'What on earth do you think he's found?' Sophie asked, as she was very, familiar with Sir Charles' eccentricities and amused by them.

'I have absolutely no idea,' I said. 'You know what he's like. For all I know he's found an old fridge dumped there by a fly-tipper.'

'Oh, come off it, it won't be anything as boring as that,' said Sophie. 'Surely he's found something a little bit exciting.'

'Well, we'll have to wait and see,' I replied. 'It will be fun if he has found something worth looking at, but I'll reserve my judgement until tomorrow.'

We went to bed early, hoping for an uninterrupted night's sleep. There was an intercom between Emma's room and ours, so that if she woke in the night one of us could creep through and deal with any problem. Fortunately, Sophie usually took on that duty and I was not going to interfere with the arrangement.

I was up early the next morning as Sir Charles wanted to meet at 7.30 am, which was his normal time for taking out his two black standard poodles, Monty and Napoleon. The poodles would cut quite a dash on the shooting field where one usually encountered only Labradors, spaniels and the odd pointer. Surprisingly they were excellent gun dogs and I understood that originally the breed had been used in France as water retrievers.

It was a cold bright January morning and there was a heavy frost on the ground. The skies above Suffolk are supposed to be some of the purest in England, presumably because of the fresh winds blowing in from the sea. The light was clear and brilliant and the sun reflected off the frost, dazzling our eyes as we set off on our walk.

Sir Charles was still secretive about his find, but excited to show me.

'Good of you to get here so early, James,' he said, 'but I like to get up and out early. It always makes me feel good for the day. By the way I do hope you will join me for breakfast as I've told Mrs Jubb to expect you.'

'That's very kind Sir Charles,' I said, 'and most welcome.'

I had had some of Mrs Jubb's breakfasts before and they were quite an event. Whatever we were about to discover, the treat of such a meal was worth the early start.

We walked from the Hall across the substantial lawns following immaculately kept wide gravel paths as far as a large raised stone pond which sat symmetrically in front of the north face of the Hall. A massive sculpture of an eagle hovered majestically above the water, the centrepiece of a magnificent fountain.

We turned and looked back at the house.

'You know, James,' Sir Charles said, 'there's not one day passes when I don't relish the beauty of this place. Jolly lucky to live here, you know.'

I agreed with him. Not only was he lucky to live there, he was also in the fortunate position of having enough wealth to keep and run the place to the highest standard. Sir Charles himself might be faded grandeur, dressed as he was in his normal attire of well-worn, threadbare tweeds, but that did not extend to his estate.

We continued down a flight of wide stone steps to the balustrade-fronted rose gardens and out through a gate into the pleasure grounds. Most houses of this size would have an extensive area of less formal gardens, usually with a collection of trees and shrubs and expanses of mown grass. This was the arboretum and Sir Charles' forebears had had it planned and planted with vision. There were hundreds of different varieties of trees and at all times of the year, although best in the autumn, there was interesting colour and form. Sir Charles was very keen on trees, not only in his woods but also in the arboretum and he had continued to collect and add to the collection.

His dogs ran on, knowing that they were free from the formality of the gardens, and put up the odd pheasant or two that had taken refuge in some of the bushes.

At the far end of the arboretum we crossed a

bridge over a small stream and then took a path alongside a grass field. The field was empty of stock but for much of the year Sir Charles' brood mares grazed there and he would come down in the morning to see them. At this time of the year they were kept nearer the stables.

'It's not far now,' Sir Charles assured me. 'In fact it's in the next field, about halfway down the headland.'

I looked across to where he was vaguely pointing. The next field had been ploughed following a failed crop of sugar beet and clearly the farm manager had taken advantage of the frost to get on the land.

We reached a stile and I stood aside to let Sir Charles cross it. He handed me his thumbstick to hold, a beautifully polished shaft of holly, with a deer horn handle.

'Age before beauty, eh?' he joked, as he mounted the stile.

The smile was soon wiped off his face, as with a sickening crack, the plank gave way and the baronet came crashing down astride the top rail. He then sort of slithered off the far side and collapsed in a heap on the ground, clutching his balls.

I muttered some condolences and took a few steps away, allowing him some dignity whilst he recovered. Monty and Napoleon arrived to investigate the commotion by which time Sir Charles was regaining his composure. I clambered over what was left of the stile to help him up and return his thumbstick.

There was a considerable amount of anguished

muttering, mostly consisting of bloody this, and bloody that. Once Sir Charles was back on his feet we started off slowly down the edge of the field. He clearly did not want to discuss the matter further but suddenly he turned around and exclaimed, 'Damn painful that!' before walking on. For him there was no more to discuss and that was the end of the matter.

A few hundred yards down the field a piece of hazel was sticking out of the plough. This was where Sir Charles led us. The furrows were hard and frozen with the frost, the sides that were exposed to the sun just beginning to thaw.

'Over here,' he said, pointing with his stick, 'this is where I found it. I think we might have quite a discovery here you know.'

I looked where he was pointing but all I could see was the hazel stick he had used as a marker.

I must have appeared nonplussed as Sir Charles went on, 'You've got to look closely, very closely. In fact I only saw this because of the way the sun caught a reflection. Look, I'll show you.'

He squatted down, somewhat gingerly, and ran his hands over the plough furrow and then picked something up. It was still highly unclear to me what he had found, and it must have been an extreme moment of good luck to have found what he did. He turned and held out his hand. In it was a small, flat, round object, which could have been a washer from some piece of machinery. He spat on it and rubbed it clean.

'Gold,' he said, 'it's a gold coin.'

He handed it to me and I looked at it more carefully. Indeed it did appear to be a gold coin, completely intact although slightly misshapen, as though it had been made by hand.

'There are plenty here,' Sir Charles went on, 'and I took some back to the house yesterday and I'm pretty damned sure they're Roman.'

'Really,' I exclaimed, 'that's amazing. How many have you found so far?'

'Well, if you look carefully,' he said, beckoning me to squat down beside him, 'they're all over the place. Look – here, here, some over there, look.'

There were indeed perhaps forty or fifty coins. We both began picking them up and cleaning them and they were all similar in colour and shape. On one side of each coin there was the imprint of a man's head, together with some words that I did not understand.

'From what I can tell they are Roman, from the late fourth century, AD 375-392, and I believe that this is Emperor Valentinian II.'

My natural instinct was to return home and get some tools to start exploring further. However, I had heard somewhere that it is far better to leave such discoveries alone, and ask the archaeologists to investigate before disturbing the site.

I discussed this with Sir Charles.

'Yes,' he said, 'I think you're absolutely right, we should get some archaeologist fellow out to have a look. I just wanted to show you before we have hordes of people milling around. I always think a little excitement like this should be shared,' he said, 'but look, this is even more exciting.'

He reached over and pulled out the hazel stick and used it to scrape away some soil. By opening up a small hole in the ground he uncovered a number of other objects. He lifted one out and showed it to me. It was a beautiful intricately moulded silver spoon, with gold inlay. The handles were curved, rather like that of a swan's neck. This was very exciting.

I wished I had a camera with me to record the moment as I was both delighted and rather honoured that Sir Charles had wanted to share the discovery with me.

Chapter 8

By the time we returned to the Hall the warmth from the sun could be felt. It was approaching 9 am and I was due in the office so I asked Sir Charles if I could phone Anne to explain that I would be late. In fact it was highly likely that the whole day would now be disrupted, but before I contacted the archaeologists we had breakfast.

Sir Charles always had his breakfast in the state dining room. He had once explained to me that although it might be more practical to eat in a smaller room, he felt that if he didn't use the state dining room then he would hardly go in there.

He sat at one end of the table, which was about sixty feet long, and I sat to one side about ten feet away, which I suppose he considered intimate. Our places had been laid and on a beautiful Georgian sideboard a row of silver tureens was set out on a hot plate.

The massive room was an extravagance of late eighteenth-century design with intricately carved cornices painted in gilt and a fresco depicting a royal stag hunt covering the ceiling. It was rumoured to be by George Stubbs although its exact provenance had never been confirmed. The walls were adorned with several masterpieces, the provenance of which was certain. I knew from the estate insurance policies that there were a considerable number of Rubens amongst the immensely valuable Frampton collection. Sir Charles' paintings were, considered by many to form the finest private art collection in Europe so the room made a good backdrop for a plate of bacon and eggs. In fact, the tureens contained not only bacon and eggs but also mushrooms, tomatoes, kedgeree, sausages and black pudding. Hole was excused breakfast duties so Sir Charles was attended to by one of his footmen. I only knew the household staff vaguely as Hole dealt with domestic matters but I did know that this footman was George Stone, a young chap who lived in a flat above the stables near the house. He was dressed in the Buckley livery and came in to serve coffee and toast. We helped ourselves from the hot dishes on the sideboard.

Although it was uncommon for Sir Charles to talk at the breakfast table today he wanted to discuss what we should do about his find.

'I think the first thing we should do, Sir Charles,' I said, 'is to ring the Suffolk County Council Archaeological Department. They probably ought to have a look and then decide whether to get someone in, or whether they'll investigate it themselves.'

Sir Charles agreed.

'I wonder if we should get someone to go and stand by it,' he asked adding, 'for security sake. We want to keep the public orf.'

'Well I don't think so,' I answered, 'after all there's not really much to see unless you know what you're looking for is there?'

'No, I suppose not,' he said, 'although it would be a bit of a disaster if Bill Bailey goes in there

91

with his farm machinery.'

'Yes, that's true,' I replied, 'I will ask him what his plans are, but I think it's probably quite unlikely that he'll go in there today. Now the frost's melting I should think the ground is a bit sticky to get on.'

'Yes, you're probably right. Anyway after breakfast perhaps you would be kind enough to check with him and then arrange for these archaeological people to come over, and then let me know what's going on, will you, James?'

'Of course I will, Sir Charles. I expect they'll be quite keen to get up here as soon as they can. Are you around all day?'

'Oh, indeed, yes, yes. That's slightly why I wanted to leave this until this morning because I wasn't here yesterday, and I don't want to miss the fun.'

We finished breakfast in companionable silence, although I always felt slightly uncomfortable in such a situation. Sir Charles was a very kind and thoughtful employer but nonetheless it was a master–servant relationship.

As soon as breakfast was over I hurried along the passageways to find Hole in his pantry.

'Morning, Mr Hole,' I said.

'Morning, Mr Aden, I gather you've been breakfasting with Sir Charles.'

'Yes, and a very good breakfast it was. Please tell Mrs Jubb how much I enjoyed it.'

'Indeed I shall,' he assured me.

'Would you mind please if I borrowed your telephone? I have some urgent calls to make on behalf of Sir Charles.' I had left my mobile phone in the estate office.

'By all means, Mr Aden, do please help yourself.'

He retired from the room and I rang Anne in the office.

'Morning, Anne, again, it's James here. Could you get hold of Bill Bailey please and ask him to give me a ring at the Hall. Tell him it's quite urgent so I'll wait up here until he's rung.'

'Okay,' she assured me, 'you're still up there with Sir Charles, are you?'

'Yes, I am. I think I'll be delayed up here for a while so could you be kind and cancel any appointments that I've got for today? I can't remember who might be coming in but my diary's on my desk.'

'Oh,' she said, 'has something happened up there then?'

'Well, sort of, it's a bit early to say but I'll try and get into the office later and explain. Sir Charles has asked me to sort something out for him which can't wait.'

I put the phone down and went to find Hole, who was in one of his many rooms that led off the back hall. This was a series of old-fashioned offices needed for the running of a large house. There seemed to be rooms for everything: a boot room, a gunroom, laundries, a flower room, numerous sculleries, the odd maid's sitting room and so on. They were all still in use and contained a most interesting collection of all kinds of articles including the odd maid. As Sir Charles never threw anything away they were a treasure trove of life below stairs in a grand house.

'Ah, Mr Hole, I wonder if you'd be kind enough to find me the number of Suffolk County Council, please,' I asked.

'Of course, sir, we'll go back to my office.'

As he was searching for the number his telephone rang.

'It may be Bill Bailey for me,' I explained.

He picked up the telephone and announced, 'Frampton Hall.'

There was an exchange of pleasantries and then he said, 'Yes, Mr Aden is in the Hall, and I shall put you through to him.'

He handed me the receiver.

'Thanks for ringing, Bill,' I said. 'I've been out this morning with Sir Charles down to the field beyond the arboretum – you know, the one which you've recently ploughed after the sugar beet disaster.'

'Oh, yes, Mr Aden. I hope Sir Charles didn't mind us getting in there on the hard ground,' he explained, 'but I wanted to get on while we could.'

'No, that's not the problem at all,' I assured him. 'I just wanted to know when you are next cultivating that field.'

'Well, we'll leave it now for a few weeks and let the frost break it down, so I wasn't really expecting to do much there till March now.'

'Okay, that's fine,' I replied. 'Sir Charles wants it left alone for the time being, so I can assure him that that will be so.'

'Yes, that's fine, Mr Aden.' He seemed slightly puzzled as to why Sir Charles wanted to be intricately advised as to the cultivations, so I added,

'There's a reason to leave it alone and I'll be able to explain in a day or so.' I felt that at this stage the less people who knew about this potential find the better.

With that call over I dialled the council and asked for their archaeology department.

I got some youth opportunities worker on the phone, or so it appeared.

'My name's James Aden, agent at the Frampton Estate,' I explained, 'and I wondered if I could speak to your senior archaeologist please.'

The girl replied, 'I'm not sure if she's in. She's either in a meeting or having her coffee break, because I've just tried to put a call through and there's no answer.'

'Do you think you could find out for me please and let me know? It's really quite urgent that I speak to her.'

'Well I'll go and have a look,' she whined, 'but it's at the other end of the corridor where she might be having her coffee.'

'Okay,' I said, 'well I'll hold on. By the way what's the name of your senior archaeologist?'

'It depends on what you mean by senior,' she said.

'I mean the person in charge,' I replied.

'Oh,' she said, 'well, Mrs Evans is really in charge but she's more of an administrator than an archaeologist.'

'Perhaps I should speak to Mrs Evans to start with,' I suggested.

'Well I do know that Mrs Evans is having her coffee break,' the girl explained, 'so perhaps you could ring back in about twenty minutes?'

'I think that you'll find that the county council is supposed to serve the community,' I remarked rather brusquely. 'Frankly I don't want to wait until Mrs Evans has finished her coffee and it's suitable for me to phone back, I should like to speak to either her or your senior archaeologist, if you know who she is, and could you get them on the phone now please.'

'Well I'll go and see if Mrs Evans has finished her coffee,' she said, 'but I know it's someone's birthday today and they are having doughnuts.'

She disappeared but within a few moments was back.

'I'm afraid I can't find Mrs Evans,' she said, 'she's not in the coffee room. But I could if you like take your number and get her to ring you back when she returns.'

'That would be very helpful,' I agreed and gave her the number.

I sat at Hole's desk wondering how long I would have to wait for the call. Mrs Jubb came in and enquired as to whether I should like a cup of coffee, which I gratefully accepted. I followed her into the kitchen where several of the house staff had congregated for their coffee and mid-morning break. Much like the council I suppose, except without the doughnuts.

To my surprise, Hole appeared almost immediately to say that there was a call for me.

'Hello, Aden here, Frampton Hall,' I said.

'Hello, it's Diane Evans from the County Council Archaeological Department,' she said. 'I've a message to return your call.'

'Thank you for ringing back so promptly,' I said.

'I'm trying to get hold of your senior archaeologist to discuss a matter of some urgency with her, and I'm afraid I don't even know her name.'

'Our senior archaeologist is Miss Goose,' she told me, 'and I do believe she's somewhere in the building. Is this something I can help with or must you speak with her directly?'

'I would rather speak to her directly,' I confirmed. 'You could tell her that Sir Charles Buckley has made an interesting find on his estate and that I think she ought to be aware of it.'

'Oh, I see,' she said, 'yes, you're probably right. I will have a scout around and see if I can get her to ring you back. Will you be on this number all day?'

'No, I won't, so I'd be really grateful if you can get her to ring me relatively quickly,' I said, 'I'll wait here until she calls.'

Rather than loiter in Hole's pantry, I went off for a wander around the house. I was sure that somehow Hole would find me when the lady rang back.

Sir Charles had told me, when I first came to the estate, that I was welcome to explore the house whenever I liked. In fact I had had little opportunity so there were plenty of discoveries for me still to make.

Rather than predictably head for the grand state rooms I decided to go underground and investigate the cellars. There was a door leading from the servants' quarters passage and I told one of the maids that I would be down there if Hole wanted me. The cellars underneath Frampton Hall were extensive. I imagined that they might be similar to being underground in a mine, as they stretched seemingly endlessly along passageways lit quite dimly by bare electric light bulbs strung to the ceiling on a wire. The cellars were constructed of stone, which must have originally been brought in because traditionally the area's construction materials were brick and clay, wattle and daub. There were beautiful arched walkways with rooms leading off, each fronted by a carved wooden door. Some were solid while others had iron grills in them, presumably to allow ventilation. Most of the rooms or caverns had little in them. The wine cellars were down here but I knew from a previous trip that they were kept locked. Some areas were used for storage, but quite what they were storing I couldn't make out. I was not inclined to start rummaging around, not least because I suspected that there may be the odd rat or two lurking in the background.

I was on my way back to the surface when I heard Hole clipping along the main passage. He wore shoes with metal plates in the heels to extend their wear and it sounded as though a small pony was approaching me.

'Ah, Mr Aden, the lady that you require is on the telephone in my office,' he said.

'On my way back, Mr Hole, thank you very much,' and I followed him upstairs. I hoped Miss Goose was still on the phone waiting.

Indeed she was, although I detected a slight annoyance.

'I'm sorry to keep you, Miss Goose,' I said, 'it's very kind of you to ring me back.'

'Not at all,' she said curtly. 'What can I do to

help? I hear that you might have found something which you need to report to us.'

I could not make out whether her curt manner was her nature, or because she had been kept waiting on the telephone. Indeed, Mrs Evans at the council might not have expressed my relayed message very clearly. Whatever the case, Miss Goose did not seem approachable. Perhaps that was the nature of archaeologists who perhaps prefer, by inclination, to deal with things that are old or dead.

I explained who I was. Conveniently she not only knew, but had visited the estate in the past.

'Sir Charles was out walking in one of his fields which has recently been ploughed,' I explained, 'and has found a number of gold coins. He has managed to carry out a little bit of research and we believe that they date from about AD 375-392 and have Emperor Valentinian II on them.'

Her voice became more animated as we spoke, and she questioned me further although there was little more I could tell her.

'However, the most exciting thing,' I continued, 'is that just under the surface of the ground where these coins are, Sir Charles has found some silver spoons.'

I again tried to describe them as best I could from my brief inspection.

'Oh, my goodness,' she exclaimed, 'this could be really important. Please tell me that you haven't started to dig it all up?'

'No, I can assure you that just the surface has been disturbed. We felt that leaving everything in situ might be more archaeologically rewarding.'

'This is excellent, really, really excellent,' she said, 'in fact I think we need to get out there right away.' She paused. 'There is only a small team of us here in Suffolk,' she explained, 'and I'm not sure who is around today. What's the best thing to do?' she asked herself.

'When you've sorted out your logistics,' I suggested, 'why don't you give me a ring? I'll give you the estate office number, and then you can arrange to come over to Frampton. I suggest you meet me there, it's in the market square in Frampton. I presume you know that?'

'Yes, indeed I do. I spend quite a bit of time in or around Frampton as you can imagine, with its medieval connection.'

'Fine, I'll expect to hear from you later then, Miss Goose.'

'Thank you very much,' she said, 'and I'll ring back within an hour. By the way, is the location secret or do lots of people know about it? Because if they do I think it would be helpful if you could get someone to go and guard it.'

'No, I can assure you that it's only Sir Charles and myself who know the exact location, and I doubt anyone else will go near the place,' I assured her.

Hole took me along to Sir Charles, who had migrated to his study and I explained the result of my various conversations. I promised him that as soon as I knew when Miss Goose and her team of archaeologists were due I would let him know.

Miss Goose arrived at my office a couple of hours later. From the sketchy details I had given her she had decided that there was a high chance

100

of a significant find.

I had by now given the estate office staff a brief summary of what had gone on and even Brenda, the accounts clerk who normally appeared as animated as one of her ledgers, took an interest.

Miss Goose was not quite as I expected in her appearance. I supposed, from her manner on the telephone that she was early middle-aged, with greying hair, bony and somewhat austere. In fact she was early thirties at a guess, with short, cropped blonde hair and rather dramatic looking. She almost burst into my office as Anne showed her in.

'I am really anticipating something from what you've said, Mr Aden,' she said in a voice which was quite unlike that earlier on the telephone. 'In fact so much so that I've managed to get nearly all the team together, and they are outside waiting.'

I peered out of my window and saw, to my surprise, two county council Land Rovers and half-a-dozen or so people standing around them. In addition there was a police car.

'Are the police with you?' I asked.

'Yes,' she explained, 'as a precaution I've managed to get some cover. If this turns into a major dig then we need to make it secure and we should know pretty quickly whether that will be the case.'

Miss Goose was dressed in combat trousers and heavy boots with a thick parka coat draped over her like a tent. Although fine, a breeze had picked up during the morning and the temperature was decidedly chilly.

'Right, well I'd better take you up to the site,' I

said. 'I'll just ring Sir Charles and let him know as he wants to be there to meet you and see what you find.'

I explained to Miss Goose that we could only get partway there, as there was no track across the ploughed field. I climbed into my Land Rover and the small convoy followed me out of the village up the lane towards the Hall. The closest we could get was by turning off the lane, along a very rutted cart track which led into a small block of woodland and across a grass field which adjoined the plough.

I presumed Sir Charles would walk down from the Hall and hoped that he would negotiate the stile without a repeat incident.

I was impressed by the professional manner of the archaeological team. Almost immediately they had located the position on an ordnance survey map, taken photographs of the area and dictated general notes about the place, weather, time and so on.

Miss Goose and I walked across to Sir Charles' hazel stick, whereupon she immediately hunched over the ground and within seconds found a coin.

She examined it carefully, spitting on it as we had done earlier, and exclaimed, 'Fantastic! You were absolutely right, this is from AD 375-392 and I'm pretty sure that this is Emperor Valentinian II. This is a very early find.' She looked around her.

'Where did you say you found these spoons?' she asked.

'They're under the stick,' I explained. 'If you

just scoop away some of the soil there you'll find some just underneath the surface.'

She did as I suggested, and there they were. Two beautiful gold and silver utensils, which although covered in soil looked, to me at least, to be perfectly preserved.

She started breathing very rapidly and tried to say something. I was a little concerned that she was hyperventilating but it was difficult to be sure as she was almost entirely covered by her huge green coat. Although I didn't say so, the large green blob, pulsating with a rapid and even movement, reminded me of a surprised toad.

She turned and looked at me with an expression on her face of absolute astonishment. She was unable to say anything and eventually shook her head in disbelief.

'I'm assuming that you find them interesting?' I asked.

She stood up, holding one of the spoons, staring at the object as though it might evaporate at any moment. Her fingers were trembling and I couldn't help noticing that she had long slender fingers, like that of a pianist, and well-manicured fingernails, which were now covered in dirt.

The breeze was picking up and I was feeling the cold. I hadn't expected to be standing in a field for much of the day, otherwise I should have put on some long johns before coming out.

'I can't believe what these are,' she said at last. 'These are more than important, they are hugely significant, or at least I think they will be. Let's get the others, we need to get this site secured as a major dig.'

She could hardly bear to leave her position but she needed to inform the rest of her team. They were waiting by the Land Rovers in the next field and looked up enquiringly when we returned.

Miss Goose said, 'I think I have just picked up a spoon from the late fourth century. It even looks as though it could have been in the possession of Emperor Valentinian II.'

The others looked suitably impressed. There was a solemn air of silence as what she had said sunk in. Then she became more businesslike.

'Right, we're considering this a major dig and I want all the usual precautions taken,' she said.

Her team bustled around and collected various things from their vehicles.

The two policemen asked her whether they could now leave, as no doubt they were itching to go and catch some speeding motorists or arrest some villains.

'I'm afraid not,' Miss Goose said to them. 'In fact could you contact your sergeant and request that we maintain a 24-hour guard on this site until further notice.'

From the look on their faces such a duty did not seem appealing. Nonetheless one of them returned to the police car to make the necessary calls. Meanwhile the archaeological team tramped across the plough and started setting up what looked like marker posts.

Sir Charles appeared from the arboretum end of the field. He had come without his dogs and proceeded to introduce himself to the archaeologists. He explained how he had found the coins and listened carefully to their hopes of what they might find.

At that point, Tony Williams, the head keeper, drew up in his Land Rover. Somehow any keeper always knows when strangers are on his patch and true to form he had arrived within the hour.

'What they got down 'ere then, Mr Aden?' he asked. 'Found a dead body 'ave they?'

Admittedly with the police car there and now tapes cordoning off the area it did look a little like a crime scene.

'No, Tony,' I replied, 'Sir Charles was out here and found some metal coins and we asked the archaeological people to come and investigate.'

'Oh,' he said, 'I'm always finding bits of old metal about the place, I expect it's some bits fallen off a tractor,' he assured me.

'There is that very vague possibility,' I agreed, 'but somehow I think it's highly unlikely. Already it's been confirmed that the coins Sir Charles found are gold Roman ones.'

'Oh,' he said. 'I'd better go and have a look.'

I walked with him over to the site, which as yet was still undisturbed.

'Morning, Sir Charles,' he said, raising his cap.

'Morning, Tony, we've got a little excitement going on here,' the baronet told him.

'Aye, I can see that, sir, I hear you've found some coins.'

'Indeed, indeed I have, and we think there might be even more buried somewhere about here,' he told him.

'Oh, I see,' said Tony, who only seemed slightly interested in the event, He was very much a man of practicalities, intent only on rearing birds which he could then shoot and eat.

After exchanging a few due pleasantries with Sir Charles, he departed.

'Tony,' I said as he left, 'it is quite likely that these people will be here for a few days now, and that there will be policemen here around the clock. Just so you know if you see lights and so on.'

'That's all right, Mr Aden, thank you for telling me. I shall let the other keepers know.'

In fact I suspected that they would do a better job of keeping people away than the police, but probably by using less orthodox methods. I knew that whilst he would tell the other keepers what was going on, he would be highly unlikely to spread the word for fear of outsiders coming on to his patch.

I also decided it was time to go as I was so cold. I left Sir Charles watching the dig and returned to the office to get on with my work. However, by late afternoon, I was keen to see what more they had found and went back up to the field.

They had uncovered the remnants of a large wooden cask, and although the wood had rotted away the metal clasps on its corners and fixings were still evident after all this time.

More interestingly the archaeologists had un-earthed the first layer of what it held. It appeared, from what they told me, that the top of the chest had contained gold and silver coins and immediately below was a significant amount of these swan-necked spoons. So far they had carefully extricated fourteen spoons and some other gold implements, which they told me were toothpicks.

I watched them for a while and they seemed

totally oblivious to the chill wind. The sun had set and, although it wasn't dark, the light was beginning to fade. They scraped away patiently at the soil, very carefully using little plastic splints, so it was clear that the excavation was going to take quite some while.

If it had been me, I would have, been so excited that I would have got a spade and shovelled the whole lot out so on reflection it was a sensible move to have invited them in right at the beginning.

At 5 pm, Miss Goose called it a day. The light was too poor and, although they had some useful high-powered torches, she felt it unwise to go further. The site was secured as best they could and the police were left on duty to guard it.

I had told Sophie via the telephone what had been happening during the day and she was keen to visit with me the following morning. We duly returned and were allowed to take some photographs of this momentous occasion. This time I was well prepared in my thermals so I was able to spend a couple of hours watching the archaeologists at work. They were meticulous in their recording of the excavation.

It took the best part of three days for the work to be completed. By the end of the second day news had somehow leaked out and it was published in the *Bury St Edmunds Echo* that an important Roman find had been made on the Frampton Hall Estate. This caused us and the police some aggravation as members of the public, and particularly those interested in archaeological finds, made their way to the exact location. Despite Tony Williams' robust manner of dealing with trespassers, and the presence of the police, we ended up with dozens of onlookers on the final day.

Miss Goose had transformed from being the ogre on the telephone to somebody I felt I had got to know quite well. Her enthusiasm was catching, and there is nothing more attractive than a good-looking woman professionally carrying out her work.

Whether or not she thought I was professionally carrying out my work or not, I do not know, but she did assure me that she would keep me informed of developments once the artefacts had been carefully analysed in their laboratory.

By the end of the third day everything that was to be discovered had been discovered and recorded. The members of the public, the press and even a helicopter hovering high above, had all been and gone. All that was left was a relatively small area, about twelve square yards, of disturbed soil. It felt like a dream and nothing had happened.

However about a fortnight later Miss Goose rang and made an appointment to come and see Sir Charles and I. We arranged to meet in Sir Charles' study at the Hall as she had warned me that she had exciting news.

I took her to the back entrance where we were met by Hole who ushered us along to the study. Sir Charles had arranged for Mrs Jubb to bring a pot of coffee and some biscuits through and we sat in front of a roaring log fire discussing the find.

Miss Goose seemed a little overawed by her

surroundings. Whilst she was used to dealing with objects of antiquity, and I don't mean Sir Charles, the formalities of a grand house were clearly unusual to her. I also had a feeling that she disliked dogs, which was unfortunate as Monty kept pushing his snout into her groin.

'This find, Sir Charles,' she explained, 'is turning out to be one of the most important Roman discoveries in England, and possibly in Europe.'

Sir Charles looked delighted.

'What wonderful news,' he said. 'I am tremendously excited about this. Not only is it on my estate but, I have to tell you, I am secretly rather pleased with myself for noticing it.'

'I don't doubt that at all,' she said, 'from my point of view it is an archaeologist's dream and only a very few of us are lucky enough to be involved with something like this in our working lives.'

'Absolutely, absolutely,' Sir Charles agreed.

She went on to explain, 'In fact it is so important that the whole hoard, and it is now to be referred to as the Frampton Hoard by the way, has been relocated to the British Museum in London. The greatest experts in this country are now cataloguing and examining all the pieces.'

Sir Charles offered her another digestive biscuit. She took it between her now clean and well-manicured long fingers.

'I am so pleased to have met you, Sir Charles,' she said, 'and of course to have been part of this amazing discovery.'

We spent about half an hour in the study before Sir Charles stood up, announcing that he needed to draw the meeting to a close.

'Well, thank you so much for everything, Sir Charles,' Miss Goose enthused.

'Not at all, my dear, not at all. I am really glad that we have had this little excitement in our backwater.'

'I'll show you out,' I said to Miss Goose, and accompanied her to the door.

'You will keep us informed as to what happens to it all, won't you, Miss Goose,' asked Sir Charles.

'Of course I will,' she assured him. 'I'll keep Mr Aden up to date with all the developments and I have no doubt that you will hear from either us or the British Museum quite soon.'

Chapter 9

After all the involvement with old things it was coincidental that Mrs Lamplight should appear in the office the following morning. Anne showed her in.

I didn't know her age, nor did I want to, but she was likely to be the oldest tenant on the estate. She was extremely frail, almost to the extent of being a walking skeleton and she could only walk with the help of a Zimmer frame. However, this did not stop her from getting about the village square as she lived on the far side of it, opposite the estate office.

'I would have got to see you sooner, Mr Aden,' she told me, 'but I couldn't get out because of me cock.'

All sorts of visions ran through my mind, none of which I could associate with Mrs Lamplight in her current condition.

'I'm sorry, Mrs Lamplight,' I said, 'I'm not sure that I've quite understood you there.'

'I've come to tell you,' she went on, 'that I want to vacate the cottage at the end of the month.'

'Oh, I see,' I said, not clear why she hadn't given us more notice.

'And I couldn't get out 'cos of me cockerel. The trouble is if I let the hens in the kitchen he comes in with them and he's a vicious little thing. He does a little dance on the floor but then I can't

111

get out past him through the door.'

I felt sure that she couldn't have been blocked into her house by a cockerel for weeks on end, and was not only surprised, but also a little disappointed, that she hadn't been in to see me beforehand. I only knew her vaguely as she caused us very little trouble. Her son, whom I did know, tended to take care of her and was conscious of the fact that Sir Charles let her have the cottage rent-free. She had worked as a housekeeper in the Hall for Sir Charles' father until her retirement some thirty years or more earlier.

'I'm going into a home,' she explained, 'I can't manage the stairs any more.'

This wasn't surprising as the old Tudor cottages around the square tended to have steep narrow staircases that were often a challenge for the able bodied, let alone an infirm old lady.

'Well, it doesn't matter that it's a bit short notice Mrs Lamplight,' I said, 'I'm sorry to hear that you want to leave us.'

'Oh, I don't want to leave, I'm sure of that,' she said, 'but I can't get up the stairs to the bathroom.'

The irony was that she was lucky to have an upstairs bathroom. Most of the old cottages had a bathroom tacked on behind, usually accommodated in a later Victorian addition. I was quite sure that Sir Charles, with his strong desire to look after both current and past employees, would not want her to leave the village.

'Well before you make any decisions, Mrs Lamplight,' I suggested, 'perhaps there's a possibility that we could put a bathroom in downstairs for you.'

'Well I don't know where you'd put it,' she squawked, 'I've only me front room and the kitchen as it is.'

I wasn't sure of the exact layout of her cottage, and maybe she was right, there was nowhere to put it. However, I thought it was worth a visit to see if we could help before she moved on to the slippery slope of oblivion via a nursing home.

As it happened I did not have any pressing engagements so I was able to go and have a look straight away. I gave Mrs Lamplight a ten-minute start, because although her cottage was only 100 yards away across the square, her progress was very slow.

She had left the front door open for me and I walked in to find her in the kitchen. I was rather surprised to see that she had her chickens in there with her and her earlier reference to the cockerel made a little more sense.

'You do realise I suppose, Mrs Lamplight, that you wouldn't be able to take your chickens to a nursing home?'

'I know that,' she said, 'but them are daft old birds anyway. I'd give 'em to me son to look after.'

Her chickens were wandering around on what I imagined was once a carpet but I had seen cleaner farmyards. I wondered in fact whether she would be better off in a home considering the state of her kitchen.

I had a look around the rest of the cottage. How on earth she managed to get up the stairs I couldn't imagine. Typical of Frampton's medieval cottages, they were steep, narrow and even I needed some agility to get up and down. At the top of the stairs was a small landing with a bed-room to either side. One room was stuffed full of junk and obviously unused; the other was her bedroom, which seemed remarkably clean and tidy. Going through the bedroom I came upon a small bathroom, which again was surprisingly clean and tidy.

I went back to see her in the kitchen.

'I can see how difficult it must be to get up those stairs, Mrs Lamplight,' I remarked. 'I found them difficult enough myself. How on earth do you manage to get up there?'

'I 'ave a 'elper what comes morning and night, she 'elps me up 'n get bathed and that, and in the morning she gets me up and back down the stairs,' she said.

'That must make a huge difference to you then,' I suggested.

'It does, and she does all me shopping what as I can't get over across the road, and keeps the place smart and clean.'

I looked around the kitchen, and particularly at the disaster on the floor.

She must have noticed, as she added, 'But I don't let 'er come in the kitchen 'cos she'd start messing things around.'

I didn't think messing things around was what was really required. A commercial cleaner, fumi-gation and a skip would be more appropriate. Anyway that wasn't my immediate concern. I had had this happen before when Social Services had decided that someone was unable to look after themselves and should be moved into sheltered accommodation, whatever that was. I would have thought all accommodation was sheltered otherwise there wasn't much point in having it.

There would be little point in spending estate money on a downstairs bathroom if the local authority was intent on moving her anyway. I tactfully suggested that her housekeeper-cum-care worker came to discuss a possible bathroom with me in the estate office.

'Course she can come over. She can come over and see you tomorrow,' she said. 'I'll send her over once she's got me up.'

'Excellent, Mrs Lamplight, and whilst I'm here I'll just see whether we can fit in a bathroom should the eventuality arise.'

As I had suspected, there wasn't really an obvious place to put one. The cottage had a sitting room at the front, which was then separated by the stairwell and the dreadful kitchen at the back. The only possibility was to convert an attached storeroom, which led off the kitchen. Quite how feasible that would be within the constraints of both expenditure and building regulations would take a bit more investigation.

'Do you want a cup of tea, Mr Aden?' she asked as I emerged from her lean-to storeroom covered in cobwebs.

I had learnt from experience that a seemingly innocent cup of tea prepared in a kitchen like that could lead to digestive distress.

'That's very, very kind, Mrs Lamplight, but I'm afraid I've got to rush back to the office. I only came over as I had a few minutes to spare, so please forgive me but I'll have to rush.'

She seemed neither surprised nor offended. I

115

said goodbye and left her in the kitchen with her chickens.

When I got back to the office the rest of the staff were having a coffee break. Anne, who was immensely efficient and, it has to be said, practically ran the estate, was always smartly dressed and presented an air of professionalism. This was just as well as she was the public face of estate matters.

Gail would have been suitable as the public face of the estate if the estate's business had been mainly concerned with erotic films and titillation. Even on a cold winter's day she had chosen to wear a skimpy top with plunging neckline and incredibly tight leggings, which left little to the imagination. Finally there was Brenda, the accounts clerk, a timid and quiet creature with black curly hair which never failed to remind me of Sir Charles' poodles.

As a team we worked well and the balance of all our personalities ensured both a working office and a sense of interesting social differences.

I joined them for coffee and what I thought would be an interesting catch up on news. That was short-lived when Gail started to relate what had happened to her during a nightclub visit in Bury St Edmunds the previous weekend.

I couldn't really understand why Brenda and Anne were at all interested. They were both middle aged and seemingly staid, happily married women, whilst Gail, who was about forty, frequented the same nightclubs as her eighteen-year-old daughter and apparently dressed in much the same style. For my part, when I first arrived at

Frampton, the stories used to fascinate me with a kind of morbid interest. But the stories remained remarkably similar week on week, year after year.

She had started by telling us that she had recognised some chap she met in the club as having been an ex-boyfriend of her daughter. Using what I imagined to be her considerable powers of persuasion, she took him back to her house by taxi once the club had closed. For once I admit to being intrigued as to what happened next but the office door opened and Gervaise Bin came in.

Gervaise Bin was a has-been. He was one of those people who you find in every community who had done something relatively important in his life, gone past his sell-by date and retired to the country. Once there he presumed that previous form entitled him to interfere with everybody else's lives. He never troubled himself to sit on committees, or take any actual responsibilities, but delighted in stirring up emotions.

He had come in to see me about a trivial matter. He had apparently had a load of muck, or farmyard manure as he referred to it, delivered by the estate to use on his garden. He was concerned that there seemed to be more straw than manure. If he hadn't caught me in the estate office hall then I wouldn't have entertained seeing him but it was too late.

'I don't really think I've got what I ordered,' he explained.

'Well, I'm sorry about that, Mr Bin, but this really is a matter for you to discuss with our farm manager Mr Bailey. I can't get involved with it because it's nothing to do with me.'

'You're wrong there, Mr Aden,' he said. 'Overall you are in charge of the estate and all the staff and transactions that go on. I've already spoken to Mr Bailey and he wasn't very helpful. In fact he was almost impolite.'

I could imagine he was. He had a large in-hand farm to run with a number of staff and distributing manure around the village was more of a social nicety than a business venture.

I didn't want to alienate the man because he had such a canny way of causing trouble to those he disliked. I would not be beholden to him either and some careful middle ground needed to be trod.

'I am sorry, Mr Bin, but I will not get involved with this. You made the arrangements with Mr Bailey and if the delivery fails to meet your expectations then you really must take it up with him. You must understand that, although this is obviously important to you, my job is to oversee all of Sir Charles' interests and you, as a man of considerable influence in your professional life, must see this.'

I felt I was managing the situation quite well. If he continued to labour the point with me then I could assume that his previous life was perhaps not as important as he liked to make out.

'Yes,' he said, 'I do understand how senior people must delegate. This was one of my great strengths, you know, in my career. Perhaps I was wrong to bring up the subject with you but I was passing and thought a quick chat might be helpful. Still, I'll have another word with Mr Bailey as you suggest.'

Fortunately with that he left, hopefully resolved to spread the muck around his own garden, rather than bring it in to my office.

Such was the life of a resident agent. It was certainly one of variety. From the grandeur of stately homes to peasant cottages, the discovery of Roman gold to piles of manure, my working life was anything but predictable.

The next day, Mrs Lamplight's helper came in to see me. As I suspected she was employed by the Social Services, and their official view was that she would be better off in a home. I asked whether that was really to do with the stairs and the lack of a ground-floor bathroom, or more to do with the state of her kitchen. It was both, the woman said, and I detected that she would rather have Mrs Lamplight in a home, and in effect another case closed, than be troubled by reorganising Mrs Lamplight's living arrangements.

From my point of view, and that of Sir Charles, that wasn't the way things should be done. If at all possible she should stay on with a degree of independence, her friends around her in the village and her chickens in the kitchen. This may not have been in line with good housekeeping, or come to that even hygiene, but it was in the spirit of the choice of living life as one wanted.

I recounted the situation in some detail to Sir Charles when I saw him at our next management meeting. He was adamant that if Mrs Lamplight wanted to stay then the estate would accommodate her.

Sadly, before any decisions were made, Mrs Lamplight died. It was only ten days since I had visited her cottage and the closeness of it all rather upset me. But there was a rather endearing aftermath to Mrs Lamplight's story. It took some time to come about but on a piece of land adjoining the village we built a small development of six bungalows funded with money from one of Sebastian's trusts. The trust, which in effect owned the bungalows, set criteria for who could rent them: they had to be either elderly or disabled. The little development was called Lamplight Close – much better than the original suggestion, Twilight Close.

Chapter 10

The church in Frampton had an odd position. I do not mean the position of the church as a building, which stood at the top of the hill on the edge of the village. It was a magnificent 'wool' church, which had been built during the medieval period when Suffolk was one of the wealthiest counties in England. The building was so large and grand that it almost seemed like a cathedral.

No, its position was odd because the living, or rectorship, still belonged to Sir Charles and it was he who appointed the incumbent. The current rector, the Reverend Sidebottom, had been with us for about two years, having been selected at interview by Sir Charles and one or two other people who sat on the respective committee. As the living was within the gift of the estate, the church and the rector also felt very much a part of the estate rather than just the village. In practice it meant that the rector would run around at Sir Charles' beck and call. Fortunately, Sir Charles was a devout Christian and took his responsibilities to the church very seriously. He had his own pew at the front of the church and conscientiously attended every Sunday and many other specific services as well.

There was a slight problem with Sebastian's view towards the Christian faith, in that he did not take the matter so seriously as did his father. He would occasionally attend church with his wife Serena but her situation was even more complicated as she was a Baptist.

It was something that Sir Charles was concerned about because he saw that his responsibility, and that eventually of Sebastian, was as a leader of All Saints', Frampton.

The estate's, or more specifically Sir Charles', responsibilities extended to the appointment of the rector and attending church, but they did not include its maintenance or its pastoral work. Most of that came from the diocese of Bury St Edmunds but it was essential that the church received help from the community, either through generous benefactors or, as more often was the case, fundraising.

The church fundraising tended to be run by a small number of people, led in the main by a slightly eccentric little lady called Pop Baker. I do not think that I have ever met someone with more energy and enthusiasm. She was recently retired, married with three grownup children and tirelessly went about the business of raising money for the church. She was passionate about it and was forever coming up with new ways of inspiring enthusiasm.

She had been into the estate office to see me about her latest idea. She badgered anybody and everybody within a five-mile radius to help, and on the occasion she came to see me had managed a significant coup.

Halfway between Frampton and Bury St Edmunds there was a small hamlet called Thorpfield.

In its day the hamlet had benefited from a pub, shop, post office and garage. All that was left now was the garage, but it was no ordinary garage. The owner had branched out into something quite different. Instead of messing about with cars he messed about with Wurlitzer organs, which were his great interest and hobby. These were the massive, incredibly powerful and dramatic organs that used to be in theatres, cinemas and assembly halls in the 1930s and were particularly favoured in resorts such as Blackpool and Great Yarmouth, as well as in the county towns.

The particular example that this man had rescued came from the assembly hall in Bury St Edmunds and he had taken it back to his garage and completely restored it. The garage had been transformed into a somewhat primitive concert hall. I say primitive because, as far as I could tell, all he had done was to remove the cars and mechanics equipment and put in their place tables and chairs. But people would come and listen to this mighty Compton organ and the garage had built up quite a reputation. In fact, if you wanted to hear it then it was almost imperative that you booked well beforehand.

Pop Baker had managed to secure a Friday evening for All Saints to have the entire place for its benefit. All we had to do was sell the tickets.

So a massive barrage of advertising, cajoling, threatening and encouraging began, in order to sell the 200 tickets at a good price. And it worked as by the time the event came round all tickets had been sold. Through my efforts to help Pop, I had somehow managed to be seen as the organiser of the event. That wasn't the case at all, as all I had done was sell some tickets and generally lend a bit of support and make a few suggestions. Not only did we have the organ playing but also there was to be dinner provided and a bar.

Never having heard one of these organs played live I was intrigued by the forthcoming evening.

Sophie and I happened to have a house guest on the night, a friend of mine called David who managed an estate for the Forestry Commission and was shooting on a neighbouring estate to Frampton the following day. I had warned him in advance that we would be going out for dinner and a recital on a Wurlitzer organ, but nonetheless he came to stay.

I had promised to assist on the night so Sophie, David and I went up to the garage at about 6.30 pm to help with arrangements. None of us knew what to expect and indeed when we got there all we found was a garage set out with a lot of plastic chairs and wooden trestle tables. There wasn't even any sign of the so-called mighty Compton organ, let alone any food. The one saving grace, I suppose, was that it was warm and that there was a bar in one corner. Fortunately the bar had a barman and plenty of stock behind it, so we immediately ordered strong gin and tonics whilst we waited for the event to unfold.

Pop Baker arrived in her characteristically busy manner. The ladies bringing the food were on their way, she said, and we must set out the tables with this, that, and the other. We did as we were told and within ten minutes the place was transformed. The food arrived and was displayed under its wrappings, all the tables and chairs were neatly arranged, the lights were suitably dimmed and the place took on a slightly magical, almost surreal, atmosphere.

People started to arrive and Pop instructed me to man the door. Some people had tickets with them, some people didn't have them but had paid for them, some people didn't have them and had not paid for them, and I was to sort out who was who. Fortunately, David was willing to assist and we set up a little table by the door from which we administered the entrance procedure. It ran smoothly enough although for a while I was distracted by an elderly couple who came to our table, towing behind them those suitcases on wheels. I asked if they had tickets.

'I'm sorry,' said the man, 'we don't have any tickets but we have made a reservation.'

'I presume you mean by reservation that you have bought two tickets?' I enquired.

'Tickets for what?' he asked.

'For this evening's recital,' I explained.

'Well, I don't know about that,' he went on, 'but we were booked to stay here for the night.'

I glanced around me, wondering if anyone would want to stay the night in a garage, albeit accompanied by the mighty Compton organ. He also glanced around the garage, and his wife, who I think was tired from her journey, did not really comprehend the situation.

She said, 'Is there a reception desk where we could get our room key?'

'This is a church-organised evening for an organ recital and dinner,' I explained. 'Are you

125

sure you're in the right place?'

The two of them looked at each other.

'Oh, no, we're looking for the Suffolk County Hotel,' he said. 'We're staying there for the weekend.'

As all became clear I gave them directions for the hotel, which in fact was a further mile down the road.

Meanwhile, David had procured a bottle of red wine. I sat down beside him and filled our glasses.

Sophie came over and, noticing the bottle, asked who was driving home.

'I will, if you want,' she said. 'I'm not really in a drinking mood so if you two want to scoff that then I'll stick to water.'

David and I didn't have a problem with that and gratefully enjoyed some more wine. In retrospect, however, that was a mistake. We sat down behind the table, greeting people as they came in and either taking their tickets or collecting money. Soon, 200 or so people filled the garage, and the bar was doing a roaring trade.

At 8 pm, the buffet supper was uncovered and people started queuing for their food. I thought it polite to let everyone else get theirs before we ventured forth but our bottle of wine was empty so I bought another from the bar.

By the time most people had got their supper and sat down I was beginning to wonder when the mighty Compton organ was going to appear, and from where. More immediately I was about to suggest to David that we should have some food, not least to soak up the wine, when Pop came scurrying over.

'We're about to start,' she said. 'Harry Tonks is down in the pit and is ready for the off.'

'Excellent,' I said. I presumed Harry Tonks was the organist but I wasn't quite sure what was the pit.

'What do you mean, he's in the pit, Pop?' I asked.

'Ooh,' she said, 'I thought you'd realise, the organ's down in the old engine pit and the floor opens, and the organ rises out of the ground,' she said. 'It's very impressive. I thought you had seen this before?'

'No, no, I've never seen it. In fact I was wondering where the organ was. I imagined it was behind those curtains at the back of the garage.'

'Oh, no, no, that's just to blank out the windows,' she explained.

'Oh, I'll look forward to this then.'

I sat back down in my chair next to David.

'No, don't sit down,' Pop told me, 'you've got to come and do the announcements.'

I must have looked rather alarmed, as she continued, 'Well, you're the best person to do it. You're one of the organisers and without you it wouldn't have happened.'

I suspect it would have happened with Pop's driving force, whether or not I was involved. However, my frantic glance around the room made me realise that no one else was likely to do the welcome. I stood up, a little unsteady from the wine, and was ushered on to the stage.

Somebody who was something to do with the organ handed me a microphone. I do not mind public speaking but only if I'm prepared. This

127

time I was not only not prepared, but had had only two minutes' warning and the best part of a bottle of wine.

I did what I could.

'Ladies and gentlemen,' I bellowed across the garage, 'welcome to this wonderful evening in support of All Saints, Frampton, and I hope that you all have a wonderful evening. We are indebted to you all for c-coming h-h-here this evening, and also to our wonderful gaggle of ladies who have prepared your meal. I am schertain, schert, certain that above all you must be indebted to ... Hairy ... Harry Tonks, who will be playing the mighty Compton organ. Quite where his organ is, I have no idea but, ladies and gentlemen, let's take it away!'

The stage on which I was standing began to vibrate a little and, much to my amazement, as part of it opened up there was a blast of music and the mighty organ rose from its pit on to the stage. The organ was not only a sound machine but also a kaleidoscope of multicoloured lights. This huge thing was flashing and bellowing like some futuristic object from a faraway planet in a distant galaxy. This strange apparition was not a result of drinking too much wine too quickly but very real. From my prominent position at the side of the stage I could see the audience mesmerised by the unfolding dramatic appearance. Some of the audience clapped in applause, others, like me, were so startled we stared with open mouths.

It was certainly time for me to leave the stage, which I did so rather abruptly as I missed the little ladder and fell headlong on to the floor.

Fortunately most people were more interested in Mr Tonks' organ, so I was able to scuttle away and rejoin David and Sophie by the door.

The evening turned out to be a huge success and raised a considerable amount of money for work on the church. And it wasn't long before Pop came up with a sensible moneysaving idea. One of the congregation, a Mr Partridge, who lived in the village, kept two or three sheep in a little paddock behind his house. Once they had lambed he found himself with eight sheep and not enough grass. Pop suggested that he should graze them in the churchyard. It was a brilliant idea and welcomed not only by Mr Partridge but also by most of the people who attended the church. They all thought it was far better to have some sheep there than a chap coming once a week with a noisy petrol lawn mower.

As Sophie and I had a sheep farm, Mr Partridge relied on me for the occasional bit of expert advice. I wasn't sure that expert advice was what I could give but I did have plenty of practical experience when it came to looking after sheep. Mr Partridge's method of looking after them was not at all similar. Under no circumstances would one have called it a commercial operation in either scale or approach.

He asked me to go and help him move four young ewes from his paddock behind his house into the churchyard. His wife, it seemed, considered his sheep hobby his own business. She had no inclination to assist with his flock mastering although was very happy stocking her freezer with home-grown lamb.

In view of Mr Partridge's assistance to the church I felt obliged to help. So I duly arrived one morning at his house to help move the sheep. I had expected to find the sheep penned up and a Land Rover, or something similar, conveniently nearby. That was not the case. The sheep were in the paddock and there was no sign of any useful means of conveying them the half-mile or so up the road.

'Good morning, Mr Partridge,' I said. 'Are you still on for moving these sheep up to the church-yard?'

'Oh, yes, James, it's terribly kind of you to come and help. I really couldn't do it without you. It's the devil of a job finding someone and it would be a bit of a struggle on my own.'

'I expect it would,' I agreed. 'Are these the sheep you want to move?'

'Yes,' he said, 'we're taking four of them up to the church and leaving four here.'

'Oh, right,' I said, 'where are you going to pen them in?'

'Oh, I don't need to pen them in,' he explained, 'I just get a bucket of feed and they'll come run-ning up to me.'

'And then what do we do with them?' I en-quired.

'Well, I just put them in the back of my car and we'll take them up in that,' he said.

I looked at his car, which was a Ford Mondeo estate, and supposed that would be as good as anything provided we didn't have to leave the tarmac.

'What I tend to do,' he explained, 'is drive my

car into the paddock and then by the shed there get the sheep to congregate, and I thought we could perhaps just lift the four in that we want and drive off from there.'

'I suppose if they're tame then we can do that,' I said, 'but it's on a bit of a slope, don't you think your car might get stuck?'

'Oh, no, I don't think so,' he said. 'I have done this before, although perhaps not when it's been quite so rainy but I think we'll be all right.'

He duly drove his car close to the appointed shed and he was quite correct, the tame sheep were relatively easy to catch and bundle into the back of his car.

'I'll open the gate and let you drive out,' I suggested.

'Excellent, thank you. I'll take a bit of a sweep round so as not to get stuck and then you can jump in once we're on the driveway again.'

I watched as Mr Partridge spun his car in a semicircle on the paddock. He achieved a graceful sweep, carving an elegant brown crescent through the grass. Clearly the car wasn't going anywhere.

Mr Partridge got out, slightly flustered.

'It seems as though it's a little stickier than I thought,' he explained. 'Can't get up the bloody slope to the driveway now.'

The sheep were peering through the back window of his car, flummoxed as to why their owner should be spinning them around for no obvious reason.

'Not all's lost though,' he said. 'I'm allowed to go out of the paddock at the bottom through my neighbour's field.'

Mr Partridge was in his late fifties and worked for a building society in Bury St Edmunds. He gave the air of being somebody who thought he was in control of the situation even though he was clearly completely out of his depth.

I sauntered off to the other end of his paddock and opened a somewhat rusty old iron gate, which relied on the dreaded string rather than hinges as its means of support. Slowly, Mr Partridge drove his Mondeo estate car down the slope and through the gateway. After I had closed the gate he beckoned me to get in so that we could drive across the field to the lane at the bottom. I looked across the field and I have to admit the slope seemed rather alarming. Even in Suffolk there were such things as hills and this was most definitely one of them.

'Are you quite sure that your car is going to get down here?' I asked.

'Oh, yes,' he said, 'I've done this many times before. Quite often it's easier to get out this way because of the weight of the sheep in the back.'

I wasn't so sure. It was a grass field but there was no obvious track and it had been raining for the past few days so the ground was sodden and slippery.

'Come on, James, get in. We just take a line across the side of the hill and then turn towards the gate at the bottom. Don't worry, I've never had a problem doing this before.'

With some trepidation I got in the passenger seat and we set off. To be fair, Mr Partridge drove extremely slowly but his planned course of direction very soon proved impossible. The car started sliding and he did the worst thing possible in the circumstances. He started to brake. The result was that the car started sliding sideways down the hill, completely out of control, with a rather desperate Mr Partridge flinging the steering wheel this way and that and braking so hard that I thought he might snap the pedal.

We were now careering sideways down a hill in a Ford Mondeo, with no apparent means of averting catastrophe. At one point, Mr Partridge shouted, 'Hold on, I think we're going to roll,' and I, and presumably the four sheep in the back, braced ourselves for the worst. The car slithered and bumped at an alarming angle but in seconds it was all over. We had come to a standstill on a slightly flatter piece of ground, the car still upright.

Mr Partridge seemed to regain his composure almost immediately

'That was a bit of a scare,' he said. 'Doesn't usually do that. Still, a straight run for the gate now then eh?'

And off we went, this time in a direct line. It was with some considerable relief that I got out of the car and let him on to the lane as I realised that just the tiniest difference in the terrain or slope of the hill would have caused the car to roll over. And all for the sake of putting four sheep into the churchyard.

More drama was to unfold when we finally reached the churchyard. Mr Partridge backed his car as near as he could to the gate, and despite my suggestion that we should get some barriers to stop the sheep running off down the road, he was quite adamant that they would follow him into the churchyard. They didn't. They took off down the street no doubt stirred up by the excitement of their ride down the hill. There really wasn't much I could do. Mr Partridge was shouting quite un-Christian things from the churchyard, while his four semi-domesticated sheep had disappeared down Church Street.

He came rushing back out and jumped in the car.

'Quick,' he shouted, 'we'll go after them.'

We raced down the road with the boot still open until we caught up with the sheep which had been stopped by some people walking up the road. Both the people walking up the road and the sheep seemed unsure of what to do next. This was Mr Partridge's chance.

He leapt from the car with a bucket of sheep nuts and fortunately the animals recognised both him and the tantalising smell of their feed and followed him back up the road into their new home.

Chapter 11

Sir Charles was patron of the Eastern Shires County Agricultural Society, which held the County Show each year and was considered to be the most important show of its kind in Suffolk. The society had a long history, dating back to 1780, and one of the Buckley baronets had always been patron. It was considered an honour. Whether the honour was bestowed upon Sir Charles or upon the society depended on whose view you took.

Early in March the society held its annual general meeting, partly in preparation for the show which was to take place in July. They made a bit of a 'do' of it and held a smart luncheon in the glass-fronted pavilion on the showground near Ipswich, and all the local grandees would attend. A few of them were aristocratic land-owners, several Suffolk farmers and an increasing number of wealthy businessmen who, I suspect, saw it as a networking opportunity.

It was not particularly a matter for me but I knew a little about it because Anne tended to deal with the secretarial side for Sir Charles.

However, this year I was invited – that is I was invited to drive Sir Charles to Ipswich; Sir Charles never drove further than Bury St Edmunds on his own and would usually get Hole to drive the car any distance greater than ten miles from Framp-

135

ton Hall.

Anne put Sir Charles through on the telephone.

'James,' he said, 'I wonder if you would be so kind as to take me to Ipswich for the Eastern Shires Society AGM next Tuesday. I'm afraid that Hole has a small medical problem that needs attention and he is booked in to have it sorted out the same day.'

'I'm sure that will be fine, Sir Charles. I'll just check my diary whilst we talk.'

There was nothing particularly important booked for that day except for a visit to a sawmill that bought timber from the estate, and that was conveniently near to Ipswich. I could fit both duties in together.

'That's fine, Sir Charles,' and I explained about the sawmill visit, 'so in fact it will save a trip.'

Hole, who hated anyone driving Sir Charles' car, apart from either himself or the baronet, nonetheless had it ready outside the house on the due day. As ever, it was immaculate, the paintwork was buffed so that it gleamed and the chrome was as highly polished as a mirror. Even the timber on the rear half of the vehicle appeared to have been recently varnished. Hole, with great misgivings and cursing his ill-timed appointment at the hospital, passed me the key.

'Sir Charles never likes to proceed at more than 50 miles per hour,' he informed me, 'and when you arrive at the pavilion you must draw up in a clockwise direction so that Sir Charles' door is closest to the pavilion steps.'

'Very good, Mr Hole,' I assured him, 'I think I

can manage that.'

'And it's very important to remember,' he carried on, 'that you mustn't exceed 20 miles per hour in third gear, otherwise the car begins to shudder.'

'Oh,' I said.

'Sir Charles doesn't like the car to shudder,' he added. I sometimes wondered whether Hole had enough to occupy himself with at the Hall but in reality he had a substantial staff of domestic servants under his control so it was perhaps impressive that these minor details never escaped his attention. I suspect that Sir Charles valued Hole in great part because of this very fact.

Although Sir Charles stood on formality and, whenever Hole drove him, expected him to open the passenger door, allowing him to get out, he did not think it was appropriate for his agent to do so. He opened the car door himself.

We set off to Ipswich and I was mindful of Hole's instructions, although either we never reached a piece of road on which to accelerate above 50 mph, or quite possibly the car wasn't capable of doing 50 mph. I did notice, as we were driving across the fresh uncluttered Suffolk countryside, that we seemed to be followed by a vague though distinctive cloud of smoke. I did not consider it of much concern until we reached Ipswich and were climbing a very small hill up from the main road on to the showground where the pavilion was situated. This slightly testing hill, if it could be called a hill, caused the car to bellow great belches of thick black smoke. Sir Charles seemed not to have noticed but I had the advantage of the rear-

137

view mirror. In fact he was commenting on various aspects of the forthcoming AGM as we drove across the showground.

'Look at all these expensive cars,' he pointed out, as it appeared that most of the other guests had already arrived. There was a sprinkling of Range Rovers, some flashy sports cars and even a Bentley.

'I mean,' he said, 'these chaps must be so rich to be able to afford motor cars like these.' He gesticulated vaguely at the assembled vehicles.

I recognised one or two: a Range Rover belonging to a farmer near Cordwainers and I knew the Bentley belonged to a chap who had a factory that made plastic bags. Both of them, I was sure, were probably worth a couple of million.

Sir Charles went on, 'Extraordinary, the wealth in this country nowadays.'

I thought of the recent Buckley Trust valuation that I had carried out with the estate lawyers and did not comment on its £120 million figure.

As instructed by Hole, we drew up in a clockwise rotation so that Sir Charles could alight in front of the pavilion steps. I doubt if anyone saw his arrival as by now we were enveloped in thick black smoke and the car gave off a mighty bang when I switched off the engine.

'I hope you enjoy your luncheon, Sir Charles, and I shall return at 2.30 pm to collect you.'

Although Sir Charles was seemingly unaware of the curiosity his arrival had caused, I could see as the smoke cleared, the entire assembly of the society peering out through the glass front of the pavilion. I assume that he must have thought that

138

they were honoured by the arrival of their patron.

I was concerned about Sir Charles' car but I really couldn't do anything about it immediately. I decided to take the chance and make for my appointment at the sawmill, which I managed, and was back in time to collect Sir Charles.

As he was the first to leave we again had the congregated good and worthy of the society peering at him through the windows as he left. The car, or rather its engine, had deteriorated and although the bodywork still shone, the effect was overshadowed by the smoke.

Much to my dismay, and his, we only reached the outskirts of Ipswich when there was a terrific bang and the car stopped.

'Good heavens,' he exclaimed, 'what on earth has happened?'

'I'm afraid, Sir Charles, I think the car has a problem.'

I tried to start it but there was absolutely no life in the engine at all. We were not members of the AA or any recovery service, so we were somewhat stranded at the side of the London road. This was a predicament that I had neither envisaged nor welcomed. Sir Charles had clearly had a good lunch accompanied by some reasonable wine and was more intent on returning home for a siesta than loitering in the suburbs of Ipswich.

Any passing motorist would have assumed that Sir Charles, dressed in his best but threadbare tweed suit and in his beleaguered Morris Minor Traveller, was probably a poor pensioner struggling to keep a car on the road.

Fortunately I had my mobile telephone with

me and decided the quickest and easiest way out of this was to phone the estate office and get the local garage to collect the car.

'Anne, it's James here. I'm with Sir Charles in Ipswich and we've broken down on the London Road,' I explained.

'Oh, my goodness,' she said. 'What on earth's happened?'

'Well, I'm not really sure but the car's stopped so could you ring Mr Howdego at the garage and get him to come with a trailer and collect the car, and in the meanwhile could one of you run down here and collect us, please. We're on the London Road on this side of Ipswich.'

'Oh, dear, well, okay. One of us will come. It probably won't be me because I walked to the office and my car isn't here.'

Forty minutes later, Gail arrived. It wasn't entirely surprising that she had volunteered to run the mission. Brenda and Anne were unlikely to relish such distractions during the working day. Unfortunately, Gail's car wasn't the most appropriate as it was a semi-sports car with seats in the back that were designed for people with very short legs. Nonetheless it was a car, despite its startling turquoise colour, which I presumed was designed to attract attention. It certainly did that, and so did Gail. She was dressed in her normal tight-fitting blouse, which challenged the buttons that held everything together, a short skirt and some rather avant garde knee boots. The proximity of our breakdown to Portman Road, known equally as the home of Ipswich Town Football Club and the local red-light district, probably accounted for

140

more interest in Gail than she might normally have achieved.

We waited for one of the garage mechanics to arrive with a trailer, and oversaw Sir Charles' beloved Morris being loaded.

I crammed myself into the back of her car and Sir Charles lay in the front passenger seat at an extraordinary angle, which I can only presume was secured as such due to Gail's last Saturday-night outing.

Despite my suggestion that he could twiddle the knob and sit in a more decorous pose, he refused to do so with the result that he spent the journey home with his head practically in my lap. Altogether it was a most uncomfortable ride for all of us.

Fortunately, Hole was not at the Hall when we returned and I was able to leave the sad news about the car for Sir Charles to break to his but-ler. In due course it was repaired satisfactorily, the head cylinder gasket, or something or other having gone, but to this day, Hole blames me for ruining the car.

Life as an agent on a large landed estate tended to encompass all kinds of relatively trivial mat-ters. Occasionally something out of the ordinary would happen, such as discovering the Frampton Hoard. These exceptional events were usually well spaced out through the year but it was only a couple of months after finding the treasure that another odd thing happened.

We found a tramp living in the attic of Frampton Hall. This caused great consternation, not least because he had been there for two weeks when he was discovered.

We were fortunate in that, in so far as tramps go, he was clean and tidy and obviously rather clever or cunning to have made Frampton Hall his temporary home. The attics at the Hall were vast, containing dozens of rooms that were now used for storage but had been maids' bedrooms in the past when all the house staff were expected to live in.

The tramp had made camp in one of the bedrooms next door to which was a perfectly serviceable bathroom. Although it was cold up there it was no doubt considerably better than being on the street, and he had a comfortable bed, a working bathroom and plenty of books to read from whatever was in storage.

Apparently he had simply crept in through the back door on the East Front and made his way quietly through the house with no one seeing him. He must have carried out a little bit of research because he had chosen to reside in the attics above the West wing of the house, which Sir Charles did not really use. As they weren't used the staff did not clean them that often and so the tramp had enough isolation to play his guitar without anybody hearing him.

It transpired that he would creep down at night and make his way to the kitchen to steal some provisions to take back up to his room. This was how he got caught and it was a most alarming and potentially dangerous situation for Sir Charles.

The house usually went to bed by 10.30 pm, Sir Charles retiring and taking his two poodles with him. His bedroom was in essence a small apartment as it also contained a couple of dressing rooms, a bathroom and a sitting room. The only other people that stayed overnight in the house were Hole, who had his own flat in the East Wing, and Mrs Jubb the housekeeper.

On the evening that the tramp was discovered, Sir Charles had stayed up late and the intruder hadn't realised. Apparently, Sir Charles had fallen asleep in front of the fire in the library and the intruder had been heard by the poodles as he walked past. Monty and Napoleon tore out into the hall, barking furiously, causing the man to run down the passage with the dogs in pursuit. Sir Charles awoke and rushed out into the hallway to find it empty. Hole, who never went to bed until Sir Charles retired, heard the commotion rushing towards him at the servants' end of the house and was startled to see a man approaching, chased by the dogs. Sir Charles then appeared, wondering what was happening.

Hole shouted, 'Who on earth are you?' The tramp stopped and looked from Hole and then back towards Sir Charles.

'What's going on here, Hole?' demanded Sir Charles angrily.

'I've no idea, sir. Who are you and what are you doing?' The tramp, whose name we later found out was Tristan Timms, was not a particularly young man and must have reckoned that even the two old boys in the passage could have tackled him.

Again, Hole repeated the question, 'Who are you and what are you doing here?'

This time, Mr Timms made some sort of an answer.

'I've been residing in the attic,' he said.

I think both Mr Hole and Sir Charles must have looked incredulous.

'You've been living where?' demanded Sir Charles.

'I've been living in your attic, sir,' he said again.

'Hole, ring the police,' commanded Sir Charles, 'and you,' he said pointing at the tramp, 'don't move or I'll set these dogs on you.'

Standard poodles can be quite nasty things and Mr Timms clearly thought Sir Charles meant business. He wasn't an aggressive man and seemed to accept that his temporary high life was over.

Hole dialled 999 and told the police that he and Sir Charles had apprehended a burglar at Frampton Hall. A nearby patrol car arrived within minutes.

Sir Charles instructed Hole to let me know what had happened immediately.

With all due respect I didn't really need to know what was going on in the middle of the night, as it was a matter for the police and I could have been briefed in the morning. Such is the life of a resident agent that at about quarter to one in the morning the phone rang beside by bed.

Of course it also woke Sophie.

'Who on earth can that be,' she said blearily, 'ringing at this time of night?'

'Hello,' I answered it.

'Sorry to disturb you, Mr Aden,' Hole said, 'but Sir Charles and I have caught a burglar in the Hall. Sir Charles would like you to come up right away.'

'Have you called the police?' I asked.

'Oh, yes, of course, Mr Aden, and they've just arrived. But Sir Charles is quite insistent that you should be here as well.'

Oh, bugger, I thought. I was going to have to get up and drive over to Frampton. I explained the situation to Sophie, who was anyway by now wide awake. I climbed out of bed. The room was freezing as the heating had gone off. I grabbed what clothes I had been wearing the day before and went out into the hall to get dressed. I was as quiet as possible as I certainly didn't want to wake Emma up and start her crying.

Down in the kitchen, which was much warmer because of the Aga, the dogs looked a little surprised to see me. There were two dogs there, Bramble my black Labrador and Foster, who had now settled in as part of the family. They did not seem inclined to join me and stayed in their baskets.

As I crossed the yard to go and get my car, Jess our sheepdog started barking, unused to such nocturnal activity.

'Shh, Jess,' I shouted to her in her kennel. Once she had heard me and realised who it was she was quiet apart from a little whining to let me know she was ready for an adventure.

'No, Jess, not now,' I whispered, 'you go back to bed.'

I drove out along the dark, deserted lanes and was at Frampton Hall in just over ten minutes. There were two police cars outside the East Front and a lot of lights on in the house.

'Ah, Mr Hole,' I said as he came to greet me at

145

the door, 'what on earth's going on here?'

He explained about the capture of this intruder and I suspect even Hole embellished the dramatic moment. I do not remember ever seeing Hole so excited or expressive. From his initial story it would have appeared that Sir Charles and his butler had been racing around the house with a pack of dogs, intent on dismembering a particularly vile and vicious criminal.

In reality I suspected it was more a case of a pair of elderly gentlemen and a couple of poodles surprising a harmless old tramp. To be fair, the eventual scenario settled somewhere in between.

Tristan Timms was in Mr Hole's office along with four police officers. From his manner it was easy to tell that he was used to dealing with the police and I supposed that was inevitable, spending one's life as a tramp.

He turned out to be a rather interesting although sad character. In a previous life he had worked as a senior cataloguer for the British Library in London, and was an immensely well-read man. His well-organised life fell apart when he returned home one day to his flat near the library to find his wife had committed suicide. He then fell into a spiralling descent of despair, drink and then debt and ended up on the streets where he had been for the past ten years.

All this history came out as he was being questioned by the police. Mr Timms did not behave like a normal intruder – not that I had much experience of normal intruders. But he was somewhat embarrassed by his capture in Sir Charles' house and very apologetic for causing such alarm.

146

How he came to end up at Frampton we were never quite sure, but perhaps it had something to do with the renowned library.

The police wanted to get away and arrested Mr Timms so that he could be put in a cell for the night. He was allowed to return to the attic and collect his meagre belongings, accompanied by two of the policemen. Sir Charles wanted to see where he had been living and in the end all of us went up to inspect the evidence. The place was meticulously clean and tidy and it was extraordinary that Mr Timms had even secured some cleaning equipment from the kitchen. There were a few clothes, his guitar and a considerable number of books.

Eventually he was taken away and in a most courteous manner he apologised not only to Sir Charles, but all of us, for the trouble. Sir Charles seemed more concerned about where Mr Timms was going rather than the fact that he had been camping in his attic. Mr Timms did not know where he was going, apart from his night in the police cell, and unless Sir Charles pressed charges then he would simply go back on the streets.

When it came to it the police explained that there really weren't any charges to be made. Nothing had been stolen or broken and they felt it highly unlikely that the Crown Prosecution Service would want to pursue it.

In a peculiar sort of way I think Sir Charles felt the same about Mr Timms as I did when I found Foster on the main road. Both were lost, abandoned and in search of hope. More importantly, both were of sound character and had plenty to give in the right circumstances.

Sir Charles obviously reflected on Mr Timms during the night because when I arrived in the office a little weary the next morning there was a message to telephone him.

'It was very good of you to come out last night, James,' he said, 'and I am so grateful that I can call on you any time.'

'Not at all, Sir Charles, I was delighted that you felt you could call on me to assist. I do feel it is part of my job to be available at any time.'

The fact that I was not delighted at all at being dragged out of my bed at midnight was not something to admit to him.

'I've been thinking about that chap, you know, the tramp,' he went on, 'all night. In fact I could hardly get to sleep I feel so sorry for him. But I have had an idea.'

I sat in my chair, waiting for the next pearl of wisdom to be revealed.

'Yes, I think we should help him.'

I thought the 'we' should really be 'I'.

'In what way, Sir Charles?' I enquired tentatively.

'He could be a valuable asset to us here, you know. As I said, I've been thinking and he seems to be a professional library cataloguer, I think that's what he said, and we could give him a job here cataloguing the Frampton library. After all it does need sorting out.'

That was quite true. The collection of books at Frampton was valuable and important. Over time the records or archives had become outdated and muddled. It had been a concern of Sir Charles for a while but it was one of those things that was never very high on the list of priorities.

'So I think he could do the job of cataloguing our books,' he continued.

'Oh,' I said, rather taken aback. 'Well, um, er, are you sure that's such a good idea?'

'Oh, I'm totally sure. I think it's a marvellous idea of mine and also it will help the chap himself. Now, I don't want to discuss the idea, I want to discuss how we're going to find him. Do you think he's still in the police station?'

'I'm afraid I've no idea, Sir Charles, but I can ring and find out for you.'

'Yes, let's get him up here for an interview, and then we can go from there.'

I did as he asked and rang the police station but Mr Timms had been released without charge at 7 am. When I asked where he might now be found, the police had no idea except to say that they thought he might be loitering in Bury St Edmunds, looking for a suitable doorway in which to lodge for the forthcoming night.

That is why the eighth Baronet of Buckley and his agent were seen driving around Bury St Edmunds for most of the day, probably being mistaken for kerb crawlers, as we searched for a tramp.

Every late middle-aged man that we passed bore intense scrutiny by Sir Charles. He seemed not to notice the strange stares that he received in return. At one point he shouted, 'Stop the car, stop the car, there he is,' and leapt out only to surprise some poor man who was merely going about his shopping.

I thought it quite likely that Sir Charles and I would be spending the forthcoming night in a prison cell the way we were carrying on. With closed-circuit televisions no doubt dotted throughout the town, anybody who managed to link them all together would have watched a most bizarre sequence of events.

After about three hours of this charade, I suggested to Sir Charles that perhaps it wasn't such a good idea after all.

'No, no,' he said, 'I'm quite sure that we'll find him. We must just keep going.'

'Well, we may do, Sir Charles, but it is quite difficult with all these shoppers and the traffic, so I was wondering whether perhaps we would be better to come back this evening when Mr Timms and presumably any other tramps will be either out on their own or camped in doorways.'

Sir Charles looked at me for a while and said, 'Firstly, I have a feeling that you think I'm off my head and secondly, I think that's a damn good idea James. We'll come back tonight.'

So we returned to Frampton and once back in the office I telephoned Sophie with the unwelcome news that I would be back rather late as I needed to go and search for a tramp in Bury St Edmunds.

At 7 pm as arranged, I picked Sir Charles up from the Hall and we went back to the town. Although it was far less busy than earlier, people were out going to pubs, restaurants or clubs, and if anything our kerb crawling was all the more suspicious, especially when Sir Charles, still wearing his tweeds and carrying a thumbstick, would potter up some dark alley for a few moments and then return to the car.

I do not know who was the most surprised, Sir Charles, myself or Mr Timms, when we eventually found him. He had settled for the evening in front of Boots the Chemist. It was quite a deep entrance-way, which provided shelter from the weather, and was gaily lit on either side by a cosmetic display to the left and a promotional display for cold and flu relief to the right.

In this porchway took place one of the most unusual job interviews that I have ever witnessed. Sir Charles Buckley, eighth Baronet of Frampton, ended up offering to Mr Timms the job of cataloguing the extensive Frampton library. Mr Timms, who must have sensed a lifeline had been thrown to him, grabbed hold of it. Sir Charles was delighted.

I was less so. Here was a man who we knew very little about, who had no references and nowhere to live, being offered a job, not merely on the estate but in the house itself.

Mr Timms climbed into the back of my Land Rover and we set off to Frampton. Unfortunately, Sir Charles had clearly overlooked the small matter of where Mr Timms was to sleep.

When I brought the matter up, Sir Charles suggested that Mr Timms should return to his lair in the attic, but I was firmly against that. Sometimes I really could not understand how Sir Charles could be so naive. It was one thing having an intruder in the house, it was quite another inviting an unknown person to take up residence in an attic room.

I suggested that we found somewhere else.

'For the time being, Sir Charles, why don't we arrange for Mr Timms to stay in Mrs Bucknell's B&B, if she's got room?'

'Oh,' he said, 'well I suppose so. We'll have to ask her.'

'Is that all right with you, Mr Timms?' I asked.

Mr Timms, who was somewhat bewildered by the turn of events, meekly agreed.

With that we stopped off at Mrs Bucknell's in the village and asked if she had any vacancies. She did and with Sir Charles' promise to foot the bill he was temporarily accommodated.

In due course the estate lawyers carried out what checks they could on Tristan Timms and his background. Sir Charles then formally offered him a two-year contract to catalogue his library and I was able to find him some accommodation on the estate. There were no cottages in the village but there was a perfectly pleasant flat in the stableyard near the house, which he accepted with delight.

Tristan Timms turned out to be an asset and has remained in Sir Charles' employment. The tramp discovered in the attic and caught by the poodles is now just one of the famous stories of the Frampton estate.

Chapter 12

Back to more mundane matters: Bert Munday told me that he had an abscess on his foot. But it wasn't just his abscess that was troubling him. He had a leaking roof on his estate cottage and wanted me to help. If he hadn't had an abscess on his foot then he would have got a ladder and dealt with the matter himself.

'Fine, Bert ... well I'm sorry about your foot and I'll see what we can arrange about the roof. I'll put it on Tony's list of things to do.'

'Kind of you, Mr Aden, very kind of you. I'll leave it to you then, Mr Aden, I'll leave it to you.'

He always said everything twice. Perhaps he hadn't been listened to when a small child.

'Goodbye then, Mr Aden, goodbye then, I'll be off now. See you then, I'll be off,' and with that he limped out into the square.

Tony was our jobbing builder who carried out most of the small maintenance jobs on houses throughout the estate. In emergencies he would tend at the Hall but he was one of those builders who are generally referred to as 'bodgers', which was all very well if you were working on Bert Munday's roof or unblocking a spinster's drain, but not so reassuring when attending to the Adams marble fireplace in the state drawing room.

At the house we engaged an extremely competent and correspondingly expensive firm of builders who were regarded as craftsmen. They had on their books all the requisite trades including, when one needed, such people as marble carvers or gilt paint restorers.

Tony tended to use polyfilla and magnolia emulsion and even the cottage tenants occasionally saw through his veneer of professionalism, realising that he merely pretended to know what he was doing.

We kept him on because he was prepared to do just about anything, legal or not, to do with the building trade. In a village like Frampton with its antiquity and irregularities all kinds of property maintenance problems occurred and Tony was worth having around. If he didn't know what to do then it didn't seem to matter. He would just plunge ahead anyway and by a stroke of good luck or sheer perseverance solved most of the problems.

Quite short and stocky with a bald head, he was also a jolly amiable chap, eternally on a mission to please. The tenants liked him in the main and he was especially good with the elderly, who trusted him in their houses. He drove around the village in a large white van with a huge array of ladders, pipes and oddities strapped to the roof. At one point he assured me that he was quite capable of carrying out minor electrical repairs but when put to the test his assurance was found wanting.

Fortunately the trial took place in the estate office and was a menial little job of dealing with a socket in Gail's office. It didn't work before he arrived and it didn't work after he left. In between,

Gail received an electric shock and watched the demise of her computer.

He had then set off for Cordwainers Farm to attend to a leaking pipe in the lambing shed. We were now fully engaged in lambing the main flock, which was our busiest time of year. Some problem had occurred with the water troughs in the lambing shed and I was reasonably confident that even Tony could fix that, and in any case messing around with water pipes was rather less lethal than with electric wires.

If he was amateurish at his job, one had to respect his professionalism at the bookmakers. Tony had an excellent knowledge about horse racing and he would often spend ages discussing the topic with Sir Charles.

Sir Charles kept horses in the stables up at the Hall, one or two for hunting but his main passion was for the stud breeding racehorses. Occasionally one of his youngsters would become a winner, much to his delight and the relief of the estate accountants. Breeding racehorses seemed to be an extremely expensive hobby and even with a few winners the cost of running the stud was enormous. He had about forty horses up there, ranging from stallions and brood mares to young stock and apart from one of these occasional winners, all they did was eat, require the vet, farrier and the services of an innumerable number of grooms. It was one of those eccentricities of Sir Charles' that I had become used to – quite willing to spend well over £200,000 a year on his horses and yet insisting on remould tyres on his car

Now and then he would invite Sophie and

155

myself to a day at the races. This year was particularly exciting as he had a runner in the Gold Cup at Cheltenham and had invited a number of people to be his guests in a box on the main stand. Sir Charles always attended for the whole festival but Sophie and I were only due on Gold Cup day. We decided to make a decent event of it and arranged for our housekeeper, Mrs Painter, to look after Emma. We left early to be there in good time and had booked a place to stay in a guesthouse in Cheltenham. It wasn't the poshest place to stay but the whole of Cheltenham was booked.

We had a fantastic day at the races – a superb lunch hosted by Sir Charles in his box, very good company and some luck with the horses. Sir Charles was particularly thrilled when his horse finished third in the Gold Cup itself and the champagne flowed. His extravagance was in vivid contrast to his lifestyle at home in Frampton.

We were also joined by Sebastian and Serena and I was interested to notice that out of all the estate activities they were most enticed by the stud. It was just as well that Sir Charles planned to leave a large enough legacy for them to pursue this rich man's sport.

Sebastian, as usual, was fairly reticent and kept in the background but Serena, a former model and an extremely striking looking woman, had no such reservations. She was extremely popular with Sir Charles' guests and when out in the members' enclosure, or by the rails, attracted a lot of attention. It was clear to me that Serena's influence on Frampton in the future was likely to

156

be considerable.

I remarked on this to Sophie later that evening and she agreed it likely that the different approach that Serena would adopt would drag Frampton into the modern age, whether it liked it or not.

The two girls were quite good friends through their connection with the estate and would occasionally have lunch together. I had cautioned Sophie that it was always difficult for an agent and his family to feel on an equal footing with those of their employers. Although Sophie had inherited Cordwainers Hall and its farm, and had a reasonable private income of her own, it was nothing like the inheritance of the Frampton Hall Estate, the title and the status that went with it.

After the excesses of Sir Charles' generous and uncharacteristic entertaining, our guesthouse seemed rather plain. However, it was a perfectly acceptable place to stay with a decent bedroom, clean cotton sheets and, most importantly, an exceptional full English breakfast in the morning.

English breakfasts were giving me some concern at the time because we could never find any decent bacon. It seemed to me that no sooner had we located a good supplier than they either changed their recipe or went bust.

I broached the subject with Sophie.

'You know that Hartup Fine Foods has gone bust?' I asked her.

'No,' she said, 'I'm surprised at that. Their food was absolutely delicious. They did all those wonderful cheeses and hams, bacon, sausages and so on. How on earth could they go bust?'

'Well I'm not sure but anyway they've gone out of business, so I'm afraid we've lost our bacon supplier yet again. You know I was thinking that the best way round this is to have our own pigs.'

We had a good supply of fresh free-range eggs on the farm from the hens that clucked and scratched their way around the yard, and bread was no problem because I collected that daily from the baker in Frampton.

'Yes, I think we should have a couple of pigs and then we can fatten them up and cure some decent bacon to our own recipe,' I went on.

'Well I don't mind that,' she said. 'I mean it's hardly going to make any difference to our work on the farm. If we're not there the Flatts can feed them and actually it would be a good thing because they can eat all the kitchen scraps.'

So we decided to get a couple of Gloucester Old Spot weaners. The Gloucester Old Spot is a traditional breed and according to those in the know, produces a most delicious, slightly fatty meat excellent for curing into bacon.

It took me a while to find a breeder of Gloucester Old Spots. The problem was not that it is a comparatively rare breed as there seemed to be plenty of herds registered on their website but that none of them had available weaners to sell. It took a couple of months but eventually I was put in touch with a breeder up in Norfolk.

One Sunday morning, Sophie and I set off with clear directions and a wad of cash.

Once we reached Norfolk it became apparent that the directions were not at all clear and we spent ages driving down country lanes looking for Hillside Farm. The idea of a hillside farm in that part of Norfolk seemed implausible to me as the countryside was as flat as the proverbial pancake. Eventually, after conversing with several locals who all gave us contrasting directions, we arrived at our destination.

Even calling it Bankside Farm would have been pushing it a bit but there it was – a redbrick bungalow surrounded by copious amounts of corrugated iron sheeting, rusty farm machinery and a lot of mud. Out of all this appeared a most jovial woman with a ruddy round face and clear, sparkling eyes. Quite possibly we were the first people she had seen for some days.

She was certainly expecting us and we were ushered in with enthusiasm to see her pigs. And there were masses of them. Every shed, barn and paddock was full of pigs and they were all Gloucester Old Spots.

I don't know what it is about people who live surrounded by mess, but they are very often some of the most optimistic people one will ever meet. Mrs Banham was certainly an optimist. Despite the heavy rain and rather a cold wind off the North Sea she chatted for ages about each pen of pigs that we saw. Sophie and I were properly dressed for the inclement weather but after we had been introduced to the eighth family of pigs I was becoming a little impatient.

As we stepped around puddles of pig wee and mud and climbed over barrages of rusty corrugated iron sheets, I was tempted to think that Mrs Banham thought we had come for a day out. The general appearance of the place bore no resemblance to the health and happiness of her stock. Everything seemed in fine condition, with clean straw beds, fresh drinking water and plenty of food.

'These'll be the ones you're after then,' she said in a broad Norfolk accent.

I looked into the pen that we had now approached. There were about thirty eight- or ten-week-old weaners snuffling about in the straw. They looked very happy and clean and clearly delighted to see Mrs Banham.

'Well, they certainly look good and healthy,' I agreed.

'We would be very happy to buy a couple of these off you.'

'That's as be you would,' she remarked. 'These is some good pigs, what'll be soon off to market, so you're as welcome to have a couple of these as send 'em there.'

This seemed promising and before long Sophie had identified a couple that she particularly liked.

Mrs Banham climbed into the yard and with a swift practised stroke grabbed one of the piglets by its hind legs. It gave out the most ear-splitting squeal as though it was about to meet an untimely and gruesome death. Sophie, who despite her farming background was not used to pigs, became possibly even more distressed than the piglet.

'Can't you pick it up like a cat?' she enquired.

Mrs Banham, who by this time had got the pig dangling by its hind legs, looked at Sophie with concern. I suppose that for somebody who

160

carries pigs around by their back legs daily the noise becomes unremarkable.

'You always pick 'em up like this, me dear,' she said, 'and I never heard of anyone carrying a pig like a cat.'

The animal was loaded into the back of the car and the performance began again with the second piglet. That too was loaded into the back of the car and after the exchange and return of some banknotes we were ready to leave.

At this point, Mr Banham arrived on the scene. He looked even more like a pig than his wife and I wondered quite how long they had been living in this remote location with only their pigs for company.

'You got a couple of pigs then,' he said in that almost enquiring Norfolk accent, which makes even a statement sound like a question.

'Yes, thank you, we have,' I replied. 'A couple of really nice weaners, thank you, which we'll look forward to rearing back at home in Suffolk.'

'Oh,' he said, 'you're from Suffolk, are you?' with an intonation of amazement as though we had travelled so far.

'Yes, we're from near Frampton, just the other side of Bury St Edmunds,' I explained.

'Bury St Edmunds,' he repeated slowly, as if pronouncing foreign words. 'I've been there,' he remarked, 'it's a pleasant sort of town.'

'Yes, indeed it is,' I continued, anxious to get away. Both Sophie and I were soaking wet and the chill in the air made the heater of the Land Rover seem most appealing.

'Yup,' he went on, 'it's a nice sort of place if you

161

like shops and that. I don't really like shops, we don't tend to go into them much.'

I thought of Sophie and her manic compulsion to rush into Bury or even London when she could, to find the latest style that she liked to wear. Not that I minded. Certainly looking at Mrs Banham and her husband I would much prefer Sophie dressed in well-tailored, sometimes extravagant creations, rather than looking like a distant relative of a Gloucester Old Spot.

I was about to make some sort of reply to Mr Banham's view on shops when a very loud, low-flying aeroplane flew in above us effectively ending any conversation.

Mr Banham stared at it with interest. The saying that people in Norfolk still point at aeroplanes was almost confirmed to my delight but sadly he simply shook hands and wandered off amongst his corrugated iron sheets.

Chapter 13

I was sitting in my office pondering quietly on a matter of some complexity. I was preparing for the annual farm rent reviews which took place each March, and although there was a formula for working out these rents, in practice it came down to negotiation with each farmer. My gaze wandered over the room and my mind began to drift. I was fortunate to have a large office, about twenty feet by twenty feet, and in it there were some lovely pieces of furniture and some very handsome oil paintings, all of which had been retrieved from the attics at Frampton Hall.

As I settled upon a particularly beautiful pastoral scene of some cattle grazing by a river, I reflected that it was fitting that this painting had stayed close to its setting. It was by John Constable and the river was the Stour, about ten miles distant. The quiet was, rudely interrupted by a loud voice coming from the hall and Anne's almost inaudible response.

I knew that loud voice from old. I flung open the door and George Pratt announced, 'How on earth are you, young man?'

He strode into my office with the absolute assurance that I would drop everything to welcome him. And indeed I did.

George Pratt was the agent, and my boss, when I worked at the Rumshott Estate for Earl Leghorn.

He had not only been my boss but also my tutor as I learnt the intricacies of managing a landed estate. After I had left Rumshott we had remained friends but we saw each other only occasionally.

George was a man of certainty. He always believed that he was in the right and was keen to air his opinions.

'Sorry about no notice and all that,' he said, 'but I had a last-minute cancellation of an appointment near here and thought I would call in to see how you were getting on.'

'George, it is absolutely lovely to see you,' I said, really meaning it. He always had an air of positivity about him. His appearance matched his demeanour: a strong, slightly ruddy face, solid but fit and today, immaculately attired in a tweed suit and MCC tie.

'Now tell me what's going on here,' he demanded. 'I've heard all about this treasure stuff you found. Jolly exciting that, eh? And how about Sir Charles: is he still up at the house, or has he let that son of his in there yet?'

'Well there's no change on that front George, and indeed I have to say that the treasure find was most exciting. The only trouble is that we now have hordes of people with metal detectors sneaking in trying to find some more.'

'Huh,' he said, 'that's the great unwashed for you. Always interfering when they're not wanted.' He had a fairly clear view regarding public access on private estates.

'Anyway, George, how about a cup of coffee?' I asked him. 'Very strong, black with rather a lot of sugar I seem to remember.'

'Ahh,' he said, 'trust you not to forget the detail. Yes, that would be lovely.'

I picked up my phone and asked Anne to prepare the necessary refreshments.

'And what's happening over at Rumshott?' I asked him. 'I gather the Earl is not in very good health.'

'No, sadly not. The poor old bugger's had gout and it's rather laid him low. It seems to have been going on now for months but of course the problem is I hardly see him so I get the Countess interfering even more.'

I could imagine that her interference was most irksome, having spent some years involved with her outlandish projects.

'So it's all the usual things really,' he said. 'At the moment we've got the farm rent reviews, which I suppose you have here too.'

'Yes, George, in fact it's what I was looking at when you arrived.'

'Interesting,' he said. 'It would be useful to compare notes on what you get round here. Land's not that much different to Russetshire I imagine.'

'No, I expect they're very similar,' I agreed. 'Ah, here's the coffee, thank you, Anne.'

She laid the tray on my desk and George, having been parading around the room, took his coffee and sat down.

'Oh, I wouldn't sit in that chair, George,' I said quickly. 'It's got a wobbly...'

It was too late. For most people the chair was adequate, but with George's great enthusiasm for everything, he had sat down too quickly.

He was now lying prostrate on the floor, the

formerly three-legged chair to one side and his coffee strewn over the carpet on the other.

'Good heavens, James, haven't you got any decent furniture in this place?' he said, clambering to his feet.

It appeared that no damage was done, at least not to him. Anne appeared at the door having heard the crash and looked aghast at the commotion. When I thought for a moment I realised that George Pratt and commotion normally went hand in hand.

'I'm so sorry, George, I hope you're all right,' I offered. 'I really should have had that chair sorted out, but it's just one of those things that I've never got around to doing.'

'No, I'm fine, I'm fine. I'm always falling about the place. I'm just sorry about the carpet.' He looked to his left and added, 'And the chair of course.'

He stooped to pick up the detached leg and remarked, 'Actually it's a very fine chair this. You really should have it fixed properly, you know, James. Buy this sort of thing in an auction and it would cost a fortune.'

'Yes, I know, in fact it's from the Hall and I'm sure we ought to get it fixed. Anyway we'll have to now because with two legs it's useless.'

Anne busied herself by fetching some kitchen paper and mopping up the spillage. She dabbed rather ineffectively, but did her best.

'I think we'll have to get a cleaner in,' she said, 'as this coffee will stain.'

'Oh, don't worry about that for now, Anne,' I said, 'there are plenty of more sinister marks on this carpet. What's more important is that we get George a refill.'

'Okay, right, I'll do that,' she said, taking the soggy paper towel with her.

'Right then,' continued George, 'where do you think it's safe for me to sit in this office?'

I laughed. 'Well, either the other chair,' I suggested, 'or the sofa.' There was a large comfortable, silk-damask-covered Knole settee underneath the window that overlooked the marketplace.

'Fine view of the market square,' he said, making towards the sofa. 'One of the things that I always say is that all us resident agents get a damn fine office, don't we?'

'That's true, George. So far I've had some lovely offices. Even as the deputy agent at Rumshott mine was pretty grand.'

'Indeed it was, and I have to say I wish you were still in it.'

'That's very kind of you.' I chuckled. 'But I couldn't stay as a deputy for ever, waiting for you to push up the daisies.'

'No, you're right, and you've done well.' Anne came back in with his second cup of coffee, by which time he had taken a comfortable position on the sofa. I sat at the other end of it to avoid the impression that I was interviewing him.

'How much time have you got, George?' I asked. 'Because I remember you once saying that you would rather like to see the Long Gallery up at the Hall.'

'What a splendid idea,' he practically shouted. 'I've got a couple of hours and I'd love to see it.'

167

'Fine, I'll ring the house and see if it's convenient for us to go up.'

I went to the phone on my desk.

'Frampton Hall,' Hole announced, as he picked up the receiver.

'Ah, Mr Hole, James Aden here. I've got the agent from Rumshott with me and I wondered if we could come and look at the Long Gallery. Is Sir Charles available?'

'I'm afraid Sir Charles is indisposed,' he told me.

'Oh?' I enquired. 'Is he indisposed enough to ask if we can visit?'

'I'm afraid he is, Mr Aden,' Hole replied. 'Sir Charles is over at the stables with the stud groom, discussing breeding arrangements to do with some of the racehorses. But I'm sure it would be quite in order for you to bring the resident agent from Rumshott to look at the Long Gallery.' I thanked him and rang off.

I relayed the information to George who, having finished his coffee, leapt out of the sofa with the same speed that he had crashed to the floor twenty minutes earlier.

'Excellent, what a marvellous idea, come on,' he said. 'I'll drive you up there, it's not far is it?'

'No, it's not far. Right, I'll just grab a coat and we'll go.'

George flung open the office door, which remarkably didn't come off its hinges, and strode into the hallway.

'Thank you for the coffee,' he shouted at Anne, who was taken aback by the velocity of his movements and the volume of his speech.

'Anne, we're just going up to the Hall to have a look at the Gallery, I expect I'll be an hour or so.'

George's green Mercedes was parked outside the estate office door at an unusual angle. It looked as though he had planned a quick getaway as although it was convenient for him as the driver, it was partly blocking what was normally the way around the edge of the square. Clearly it was of no concern to him as he leapt into the car and fired the engine.

I was wary of George's driving because, as with everything else in his life, it was all or nothing. When he had last visited us at Cordwainers Hall he had reversed with such enthusiasm when leaving that his car had ended up in our pond. This time we shot across the square and down Market Passage. It was a one-way street that we entered the wrong way but we emerged with little hesitation into the High Street.

'It's up here to the right isn't it?' he barked at me, having already started to negotiate the turn.

'Yes, it is. We just follow this road all the way to the end until we reach the park.'

We proceeded up Hall Lane and already I was holding onto my seat, recollections of previous outings in this car all too vivid. It was a mystery to me how George had never had an accident assuming, as he did, that everyone would clear out of his way.

To add to my nervousness he decided to inspect and comment upon the magnificent landscape as we approached the edge of the park. The car wandered off the road occasionally at which point he would yank it back on to the tarmac with

169

absolutely no regard for the fear of his passenger.

Once we were in the park I relaxed a little. Some occasional careering across the grass was unlikely to do us any harm and with the open expanse there was no fear of collision. We shot past the south front and swept up in a spray of gravel at the east door. Hole came out to greet us and I introduced him to George Pratt.

'What a splendid building,' George remarked. 'Very kind of you to show me the Gallery in Sir Charles' absence.'

'Not at all, sir,' replied Hole. 'I am sure Sir Charles would have shown you himself had he been here, but as Mr Aden might have explained he is having a meeting at the stud.'

Hole led the way along the passageways and eventually to a door that opened into a small stairwell. This was in effect the servants' entry to the Long Gallery. The formal route was from the grand staircase leading from the South Hall.

At the top of the stairs was another door, which I knew was imperceptible from the Gallery side. We walked through.

Even George, who was used to the grandeur of stately homes, gasped. In some ways entering via the servants' stairs was more dramatic as the plainness, almost austereness, of the servants' side was such a contrast. The Long Gallery stretched along the West Front at first-floor level and ran to 140 ft in length. Most of the time the shutters were closed to avoid sunlight damaging the paintings but Hole had kindly opened them and the light streamed through. The room itself was an artistic masterpiece with a beautiful polished

170

marble floor, four intricately carved marble fireplaces along its length and an ornate part-gilded ceiling. But of course it was the paintings that were the real treasure. There were about sixty, most of them huge canvases, and all of staggering beauty. Every one of them was by a famous painter. Reynolds, Canaletto, Stubbs, Rembrandt, Renoir and so on. Sir Charles' collection was certainly one of the finest not open to the public and George was overawed by what he saw. It was one of the first times that I had seen him literally speechless as he walked slowly along the Gallery, trying to absorb both the beauty of the work and, to some extent, the importance and value of the collection.

'Good heavens above, this is extraordinary.'

He could have spent the rest of the day there he told me but apart from the fact that Hole and I had to get on with other things, he also had another appointment.

Hole showed us back to the car and after a profusion of thanks we sped off again down the drive. A flock of crows pecking on the roadway in the park came dangerously close to being squashed by the speeding Mercedes, and a small group of fallow deer which were headed our way abruptly changed their direction.

Our intended destination was hopefully back at the estate office, although I couldn't help wondering whether it might not be the hospital in Bury St Edmunds. Happily we did reach the office and rather shakily I got out of the car and said goodbye.

'Goodbye, James,' he shouted, 'and thank you

171

for a marvellous little interlude on my day out. Come over and see us – mustn't leave it so long next time.'

And he took off across the marketplace, waving like a mad thing as he did so. Swerving to miss a couple of cyclists the rear end of his car disappeared over the brow of the hill and he was gone.

'What an extraordinary man,' remarked Anne when I went back in.

'Yes, he's a bit of a whirlwind, isn't he?' I agreed. 'A very good agent though. I often think that I wouldn't be here at Frampton if it wasn't for his influence.'

Back in my office the first thing I did was to phone one of our tenants who rented a workshop in a converted farm building where he repaired furniture. I explained about the chair and he promised to come in and collect it later that day.

I found it quite difficult to settle back into working out farm rent reviews. George's surprise visit had upset my concentration so I decided to get something to eat and then inspect some replanting that had recently been completed in a block of the estate's commercial woodland.

Hilda in the baker's two doors up made me a delicious sandwich filled with thick, particularly fine mature cheddar and some mayonnaise and salad. Rather than eat it in the office I put the sandwich in my coat pocket to eat out in the wood.

It was still March and not very warm but the sun was shining and the wind was no more than a breeze. I realised that I had not been out of the office much on the estate recently and so on an

172

impulse I telephoned the stables back at the Hall and asked if they could get a horse ready for me. In practice it was far more sensible to inspect the woodlands on horseback. If you walked it took far too much time and if you drove you tended to miss seeing things. A horse was an ideal compromise.

Half an hour later I was mounted on one of Sir Charles' semi-retired hunters, Neptune, an animal that I often rode around the estate when I had the opportunity. He was a fifteen-year-old bay gelding and impeccably well mannered. He was fun to ride, lively and alert and exceptionally well schooled.

Neptune and I set off across the park and were soon cantering steadily over the centuries-old turf. The park contained many fine examples of veteran trees, especially oaks. We reached the edge of the lake, putting up some duck, which flew off with a great flapping and splashing of water making Neptune start. During the summer we issued permits for people to fish from the banks but at this time of year it was deserted. A small white wooden rowing boat was tied up against a little wooden jetty and I made a mental note that we really ought to get it in and have it repainted. I didn't think that Sir Charles used it any more but nonetheless we ought to look after it.

I rode down to the far end of the lake away from the Hall and across a small bridge where the outlet from the lake followed the course of a stream eventually winding its way into the River Stour.

We reached the edge of the park by a wooden

173

hunting gate opening into a coppice and followed a grass ride through some ancient woodlands. Predominantly the trees were ash and oak with coppiced hazel underneath. There was the distinct smell of the earth beginning to warm and a new growth of grasses and leaves. The thorn was already in leaf. Certainly the birds knew that spring was in the air and their song filled the woods. I walked Neptune along the track enabling me to enjoy those minutes. Cantering, or even trotting, and I would have missed so much of what there was to see and hear.

The coppice was on the edge of a much larger block of woodland extending to just over 400 acres. The area that we headed towards was called Frampton Hill Plantation as it had been planted on some relatively poor land on the hill overlooking the village. Most of the woodland there was coniferous, predominantly a mixture of larch and pine. It was the heart of the commercial timber venture on the estate and despite the non-native trees and the current dislike of conifer plantations they held a very valuable place in the English countryside. The larch needles in early spring were a most delicate, soft, pale green that shimmered like a haze through the plantation. And there were conservation benefits to coniferous woodlands. Some species of birds, understorey plants and particularly fungi, relished the environment.

I turned right and trotted along a stone forestry track until we reached an area of clearfell. The previous year we had felled the mature crop of European larch and over the winter replanted it. Although the foresters on the estate staff were

174

entirely competent occasionally I would have a look at what they had been doing. This area of thirty acres had suffered badly from rabbit damage and we had paid for the area to be fenced off.

Rabbit fencing is fairly expensive as the wire netting needs to be dug into the ground to prevent rabbits burrowing underneath. I didn't know whether Sir Charles had visited the new planting but I was able to report what a fine job the foresters had carried out.

It was more than usually important for me to inspect because during the winter we had taken on a new head forester. He had arrived at Frampton with excellent references from his previous employers, the Forestry Commission, and he was adept at both managing the forest workmen and securing good prices for the timber. However, he was a bit of a law unto himself and his people skills in particular were somewhat abrupt. Richard Watson appeared to get on with people that could converse about forestry knowledgeably but had little time for anyone else. Sir Charles and I both found him agreeable to work with and good at his job, but I had seen him deal with others in a less than tactful way.

Walkers who strayed from the paths, the hunt to some extent, and worst of all the shoot, incurred his wrath if they put a foot wrong in 'his' woodland.

The estate's main concern was the relationship between him and the head keeper, Tony Williams. It is not unusual to find that the head forester and the head keeper do not see eye to eye. One

175

believes the woods are solely for growing good timber, the other that the woods are simply cover for his pheasants. In truth a well-run estate copes with both. In practical terms there is absolutely no reason why good woodland management and a good shoot shouldn't go hand in hand, and generally they do. However, the personalities of the two heads of staff were critical in determining whether this would happen or not. Our previous head forester, who had been quite elderly and happy for a quiet life, had tended to let the game-keepers more or less do as they wished. Mr Watson was not of the same ilk and there had already been some major rows, which inevitably ended up in the estate office.

The situation had become even more muddled due to family influences. Sir Charles, who loved his woods, was a very keen shooting man and his relationship with Tony Williams was close. Mr Williams had been keeper on the estate for many years so it was inevitable that a close bond had formed. Sebastian's interest was in trees. He wasn't particularly interested in the commercial aspects but he had a fondness and good knowledge of ancient woodlands and our broadleaf native species. Richard Watson was a deep source of expert knowledge and it was not uncommon to see him taking Sebastian around in a battered forester's Land Rover poking about in various woodlands. Furthermore, Sebastian was not particularly keen on shooting, and although he did attend one or two days during the season I think it was more to please his father than himself.

In effect the two heads of department had

secured their own champion on the estate, and occasionally I had to exercise great diplomacy in dealing with their woes.

Richard Watson was a tall lean man with rather long, unkempt greyish hair and a manner that effectively prevented one from engaging him in conversation.

It was this direct no-nonsense approach that had caused a great deal of awkwardness with Mr and Mrs Trehawne. They were a couple who lived in a modern sprawling five-bedroom detached house on the edge of the village, built on land that for some reason the estate had never owned. I knew the Trehawnes vaguely but they tended to keep themselves to themselves and were not involved with village activity. I think they were only vaguely aware of the surrounding estate and seemed happy enough to occupy their time within their own oasis. Their house and grounds, which must have extended to nearly an acre, were indeed an oasis, surrounded on two sides by estate woodlands. The gardens were well kept, there was a kidney shaped swimming pool at the rear and an immaculate tarmacadam driveway that led to a triple garage. Mr and Mrs Trehawne clearly enjoyed motoring as usually one or two expensive cars were parked outside the house.

During the past winter the Trehawnes had telephoned the estate office to say that they were concerned that some of the trees bordering their garden looked dangerous and asked if we would fell them. Richard, as head forester, was duly tasked to inspect them and pronounced them all to be sound and healthy. As it turned out it was

177

just as well that he did.

Despite Richard's expert advice, Mr and Mrs Trehawne kept pestering me in the estate office to get some of the trees felled.

'We really do think that some of these trees are too close to the house,' Mr Trehawne had told me.

I replied, 'Well, they're perfectly safe, as you know we've had our head forester look at them so I can see no reason why we should cut them down.'

'Well our feeling is,' he went on, 'that if they fell they would cause some terrible damage.'

'Well I expect they could but it's an unlikely event and I accept that if something is dangerous then we will fell it, but if it's not then it can stay.'

'It's not just that,' he moaned on, 'but we feel they are cutting out a lot of light from the garden and particularly from the new conservatory that we've built.'

This was obviously the cause of their recent interest in our trees. It was nothing to do with safety but more to do with their inconvenience. We had encountered this kind of problem before and took a firm stand against such requests, otherwise we would end up running around after dozens of people, attending to trees, access tracks, farm smells whatever, simply to appease them. I felt like asking the Trehawnes why they had bought a house on the edge of some woodland if they were not particularly fond of trees but the question would have been inflammatory. I later heard that Richard Watson had asked them exactly that question and the ensuing conversation had resulted in

178

a distinct cooling of relations.

Mr Trehawne was involved in some kind of semi-professional business, by which I assumed something to do with insurance or financial services. It was apparent that he had made some money out of it and his slightly arrogant approach to the estate over the trees was typical. Mrs Trehawne, quite possibly considered as someone of stature by her friends, was simply a female clone of her husband, with identical irritating moans.

Preparing a second offensive I had her on the phone shortly after her husband's call.

'I am very surprised that you won't consider taking these trees down,' she said to me. 'My husband really thinks that you should. I'm very concerned because we often have my little grandchildren staying, or my elderly parents, and it would be devastating if any of them should be injured by a falling tree. Or come to that even, you know, a big branch might fall off.'

Referring to the safety of either children or old people nowadays was seen as the trump card. Her comments incensed me, particularly as by definition it meant that anyone who was over the age of say twelve and under the age of seventy was of less relevance.

'Mrs Trehawne, I really don't want to discuss this any more. We've inspected the trees – they're fine.'

'I know you've done that,' she said, 'but how do we know you're right?'

'Because Mr Watson is a professional forester, Mrs Trehawne.' I was becoming quite exasperated. 'I mean if you want your teeth fixed you go to a dentist, or your car fixed you go to a garage. Here we are with a tree problem so we've gone to a forester.'

She was becoming ruffled. 'I think it's best if I get the Environmental Health people from the council out to have a look,' she said.

'Well by all means, you can do what you want, but I assure you that the trees are staying and we've recorded a clean bill of health on our inspection.'

Whether or not the Environmental Health people ever did arrive from the council I never heard. I doubted it because I couldn't imagine that anyone from Environmental Health would know much about trees. I thought they dealt more with rats and noisy neighbours.

Of course the inevitable happened. Suffolk was hit by an exceptional gale when the ground was saturated, and a substantial oak tree blew down. It landed full and square on Mr Trehawne's black Porsche Carrera.

Richard Watson was called to inspect the situation. But under the principles of law there is no responsibility on the owner of the tree provided that the tree was healthy and the weather was recorded as exceptional. Furthermore it was the obligation of the Trehawnes to remove the tree from their car and return it to our side of the fence.

Although I wasn't there at the time I gather Richard explained this to them but kindly, on behalf of the estate, suggested they could retain the timber for firewood. He came into the office afterwards to let me know what had happened and although he did not recount Mr Trehawne's answer, it was the only time that I have seen Richard Watson grinning.

Chapter 14

We were now enjoying the glorious weather of late spring/early summer – my favourite time of year. The beginning of this particular stage in the calendar was heralded by the bluebells. We were fortunate in Suffolk to have areas of old woodland carpeted with these flowers – a purple that glowed across the floor of the woodland with a scent that pervaded every breath one took. I grasped every opportunity to borrow Neptune from the stables, especially after work before returning back to Cordwainers.

On occasions, Sophie would leave Emma with Mrs Painter and join me. The stud groom was more than willing to find a second horse and the two of us could spend an hour or two together in the early evening, riding through the estate, having a chance not only to enjoy the stunning surroundings but also each other's company.

It was surprising to me therefore that Anne had booked a six-week holiday to Australia at this time of year. She and her husband Derek had a daughter who had emigrated and she was expecting her first baby. It would be the Australian autumn and I would have waited until their summer, but I suppose a grandmother's instincts might lean more towards the birth of a grandchild than the weather. As it was a particularly long vacation, Anne had specifically asked for it outside the normal terms of her employment. I was delighted that she could go and made every effort to show my support. Anne was the lynchpin of the estate office and I relied upon her heavily and with complete faith. A poor secretary would have made my life much more difficult.

We had decided to hire a temporary secretary from an agency in Bury St Edmunds to cover her absence. Although not conversant with many of the estate ways, she would at least be able to answer the telephone and do all the typing. We had the opportunity to interview three suitable candidates.

Our formula for the interviews was straightforward. They had to demonstrate basic secretarial skills, Anne would show them what work would be required, and I interviewed them to see how they would fit into a very traditional estate office.

We selected the three and invited them over all on the same day, allowing each candidate an hour. It was also an opportunity for Gail and Brenda to meet them so that they could have some input into the decision.

The first lady was probably the most suitable. She had worked in a solicitors' office, was in her mid-fifties and competent in the type of work that she would need to undertake. However, it turned out that none of the candidates had been properly briefed by their agency as to the culture at Frampton, and this particular woman was a raging socialist who deplored nothing more than class and inherited wealth. As soon as she walked into my office, with its fine antique furniture and ornate gilt framed paintings, I could see that she felt uncomfortable. The interview as such did not get very far because she concluded that the situation would be alien to her.

The second was better. She was a young woman in her mid-twenties, quite attractive, in an earthy sort of way, and no doubt could have done the job. However, Gail took a huge and instant dislike to her, I suspect fearing unwelcome competition in her romantic liaisons. There was a distinct similarity between the two women, although the proposed secretary was nearer the age of Gail's daughter than Gail herself.

By the time the third interviewee arrived I was becoming a little despondent. I had hoped that the whole business would be quickly settled. Anne was supremely efficient, having had years of experience in the estate office and I didn't expect for one moment that we would find an exact replacement. All we needed was someone to answer the telephone, greet people when they came into reception, type my letters, put stamps on the outgoing post and open the incoming post. It wasn't particularly complicated.

But it was a busy office so we needed somebody full time and the only people in the village who could help could only come in for two or three days, which just wasn't enough. That meant having someone from outside the village who could drive as the bus service was intolerable and seemed scheduled solely to take pensioners into Bury on market day.

As it happened the third person we interviewed couldn't drive but her son would drop her off and collect her at the beginning and end of each day when passing through to his work in another town south of the village.

Her name on the form was Mrs Paten, so I was not remotely prepared when Anne showed in an Indian woman wearing a sari. With a little difficulty I established that the 'N' should have been an 'L'. That put the circumstance into comprehension. Mrs Patel had brought with her a sizeable folder containing her references and qualifications. There were far too many to read but the general gist of it was that she had been highly thought of by previous employers, family, friends, people that she had met on the bus, all of whom had regarded her as a kind and reliable soul. Somebody mentioned she could type, someone else that she could file things properly and stick stamps on envelopes.

She was a very charming, almost regal, lady and it was impossible not to take an instant liking to her. To be brutally honest I think in many estate offices she might have been out of place but Frampton was a little different Particularly because Serena's family was originally from Somalia, many of the natural prejudices that exist in traditional English villages had been broken down by her acceptance by the community.

As Anne's departure was looming close, I decided that Mrs Patel with all her references and delightful manner was worth a try. It was a shame that we had had to get her through an agency because not only were their daily rates higher than a permanent employee, but they also charged an outrageous ten per cent of her salary to cover their administrative costs. Nonetheless I appointed her then and there. She beamed at me with a most engaging smile and a profusion of thanks.

Anne, who was sitting with us, was pleased, as I think she had rather taken a liking to Mrs Patel, and ushered her out to show her the tasks that she would have to undertake. Mrs Patel would not start work until the Monday after Anne left for Australia.

I was reasonably satisfied with the outcome of our recruitment effort, although I did have a slight concern over Mrs Patel's accent. There would inevitably be comments, particularly from some of our more jovial farmers, that their calls were being put through to a call centre in India.

However, those that mattered, and by that I mean our employers, Sir Charles, Sebastian and Serena, would have no such thoughts and on that basis I was happy.

Brenda and Gail seemed pleased at the prospect of her joining us for a while although Brenda, as timid as ever, wouldn't have said much even if we'd employed a convicted serial killer. Gail on the other hand, who always said a lot, thought she was an excellent mother-type figure on which to pour all her woes, despite the fact that Mrs Patel, fifty-two years old according to her CV, was only a decade older than Gail.

We called her Mrs Patel throughout her stay because we couldn't pronounce her first name and she proved to be an asset. After she had had a few days to settle in I asked her to join me in my office for a cup of coffee to ask her how she was getting on.

She put the drinks down on my desk and

perched on the remaining chair that survived after George Pratt's visit.

'How are you coping with the typing and phones and so on?' I asked her.

'It's very good here, thank you, Mr Aden,' she said. 'I like this place very much indeed. The people are all so friendly and I understand the work.'

'Oh, I'm glad to hear that,' I said, 'because above all we like to have a good team here and everyone enjoy their work.'

'Yes, it's very good. I look forward to meeting Sir Charles one day soon I hope.'

'Yes, well he usually calls in once or twice a week so when he does I shall introduce you. I've told him that you're manning the fort while Anne's away so he'll know who you are, don't worry.'

During the second week of Mrs Patel's engagement a party of Americans visited Frampton Hall. During the Second World War an airbase had been built locally, to accommodate the US bombers shortly after America had joined the war against Germany. Every few years a group of veterans, accompanied by their wives and other members of their families, returned to Frampton to reminisce about the past. Their brief spell in England had clearly been a significant and memorable part of their early lives.

This particular group had asked if Sir Charles would be willing to host a tea party in the Hall. Sir Charles was quite amenable to this kind of event as his parents, now long dead, had often entertained the airmen at Frampton during the 1940s while Sir Charles himself was on active service, mainly in North Africa.

The party would stay at the Anne of Cleves, which had been a favourite of the pilots during the war. Indeed many of their signatures were still visible on the wall panel by the fireplace in the bar.

Frampton Hall was not open to the public but Sir Charles was generally willing to allow selected groups to visit the house. A guided tour through the main state rooms and a viewing of the paintings was an immense pleasure, more so than many other stately homes, partly because of the quality of the contents and partly because it was, in effect, by invitation.

On this occasions Sir Charles offered to show them around himself, with the assistance of Sebastian, Serena and me. He wanted Sebastian and Serena to be there because more and more he felt that they should be seen as the heirs apparent, and he wanted me to deal with the unforeseen.

We all waited in the South Hall, a magnificent room approximately the size of a tennis court and forty foot in height. The ceiling mural was reputed to be the finest in the country. It was also knows as the Marble Hall as just about everything was carved in polished marble, apart from a Formica-topped table that had come from a transport café. It was one of those eccentric things about Sir Charles that had intrigued me and shortly after I had arrived at Frampton I had asked him why it was there.

'I always think it is very useful,' he had told me, 'to put my wet hat and gloves and so on on to if I come in this door when it's been raining.'

'Oh,' I said, surprised, 'I see.'

I doubt he pottered out of the massive doors on the south front very often and in any case, in the unlikely event that Hole was not there to receive him on his return, a few moments of something damp on the marble floor would hardly have mattered. But there it was. One of the most magnificent rooms in the country, possibly on a par with the Palace of Versailles, had a small Formica table in the corner procured from a closing down transport café. The Americans didn't seem to notice it however, and I was amused that they greeted Sir Charles with royal reverence.

'It's a real-life lord,' I heard one of them say in great excitement. Trying to explain that Sir Charles was a baronet and not a baron would have been futile. They were enjoying their day.

With lots of 'ooh's and 'aah's and exclamations of, 'How can it really be that old?' they made their way around the South Hall. Sir Charles led the party of about twenty people and explained details about the architecture of the house, the paintings and the furniture.

One courageous old lady asked Sir Charles if she could sit on a particular chair that he had described as being of 'unknown maker but dated from the early 1600s'.

'Just wait till I tell the folks back home,' she exclaimed to the admiring group, 'that my butt has sat on a chair that is over 400 years old.'

There was a murmur of amusement within the group. Sir Charles looked a little surprised, Sebastian despairingly, while Serena simply took it in her stride.

'Excuse me, my lord,' she addressed Sir Charles incorrectly, 'would you mind awfully if Denman took a photo of me? It's something I'd love to show the folks back home, otherwise they simply won't believe what I tell them.'

'Well, I suppose so, umm, if you wish,' said Sir Charles, 'but I mean, it's only a chair.'

The photographic opportunity was seized, and much to my frustration, set off a series of our visitors wanting to be photographed sitting in this particular chair.

Rather amusingly, above the chair was a very small oil painting by Rembrandt. Although Sir Charles had pointed it out, the size of the painting seemed to disappoint them and nobody seemed interested in it. The large canvases drew the acclaims of the Americans seemingly irrespective of who painted them. The Rembrandt, which was of huge artistic historical importance, was completely overshadowed by a rather plain, admittedly old, chair in which they could all sit and have their photographs taken.

The tour progressed along much the same vein throughout the house, with no particular dramatic events until we reached the South Drawing Room where Hole and some of the domestic staff had set out coffee. Also in the South Drawing Room were Monty and Napoleon, lying in front of a blazing log fire.

Again the room was enormous, elaborate, stuffed with priceless furniture and famous paintings. The dogs, who had been contentedly lying on a Persian carpet in front of the fire, were aroused by the visitors.

'Oh, my gawd,' shrieked one lady, 'they've got dogs in here.'

I was standing beside her at this point and said, 'Yes, Sir Charles is very keen on his poodles. They are called Monty and Napoleon.'

'But I can't be doing with dogs,' she said. 'I have this allergy and they always seem to know it. If they come near me I shall be having fits.'

The poor lady was genuinely distressed but it was impossible to get the dogs out of the room, particularly as Sir Charles would not condone such actions. As she had predicted with alarming accuracy the dogs picked her out to be greeted. I tried to fend them off as best I could but by this time the lady was in a state of panic. Fortunately, Serena came to the rescue. Between us, and with the help of her husband, we extracted her into an anteroom.

Her husband, a large and physically able man, more or less carried her through the doors. He looked like he kept in training, despite his age, and for this instance was appropriately dressed in sneakers and a baseball cap.

Once she was out of the drawing room she seemed to relax and her breathing returned to normal. Serena was very good and summoned one of the staff to fetch the lady some water.

'I think Doreen and I perhaps better go and wait in the coach,' her husband said. 'If you'll apologise to his lordship and maybe just explain the problem then he won't think too badly of us.'

Serena replied, 'Of course I'll do that, and I'm sure that Sir Charles would be most upset to know that you have had to cut short your visit.'

'Oh, don't you worry about that,' Doreen's husband said, 'we've had a fantastic time here and we're very grateful to the lord for his hospitality.'

'Well you'll only be missing a cup of coffee,' Serena went on. 'I think the tour of the house is finished now so at least Doreen hasn't missed anything interesting.'

I showed Doreen and her husband out to the coach which was waiting on the south front. It was only a matter of another ten minutes and the rest of the party followed.

I don't think that Sir Charles had even noticed the commotion and certainly nothing was ever said about it. The Americans wrote to the estate upon their return home and expressed delight and thanks for a memorable visit and the chance to have met a real-life lord.

Chapter 15

Sir Charles came into the office a few days later to thank me for helping him with the Americans.

'By and large, James,' he said, 'I think it went orf pretty well. I don't mind these things but to be frank with you I'm getting too old to bother with them. I'm glad that Sebastian and Serena came and helped, it's about time they started taking more of an interest in the estate.'

'Yes, I've noticed that both of them are getting more involved with the village. I feel it's important that they are seen as your successors because there is nothing worse than a disinterested or absent landlord.'

'Absolutely, absolutely,' he replied, 'and on that front I'm beginning to wonder whether it isn't time for me to move out of the Hall.'

The thought of Sir Charles leaving the Hall, other than in a wooden box, was shocking to me and must have shown in my face.

'I'm only just starting to think about it,' he said, reading my expression, 'but in a few years I'll be eighty and I would hope that by then they might have a child. I've been thinking about it and, as much as I would find it difficult to leave, I think if they have a baby I shall move out. Make room for the next generation and, for that matter, the generation afterwards. I'd still be here of course but the house is wasted on me now really. I mean

I hardly ever do any entertaining and I rattle about on my own up there, so I've decided this is what will happen.'

To some extent I could understand Sir Charles' view. He had been trying to integrate Sebastian and Serena more and more into the estate, encouraging them to take decisions about its future. They both now sat in on trustees meetings and twice a year they would join Sir Charles, myself, and the family lawyer to work out estate strategy.

'But I'm going to leave it until they have a child,' he continued, 'so no immediate changes, but I thought in passing I should let you know my thoughts.'

'Have you discussed this with them?' I asked.

'Yes, a bit on and orf, but they've invited me down to their house this evening for dinner and I want to broach the subject then. It's all drifting a bit at the moment and I rather wish they would just get on and mate, as it were.'

Sir Charles, who was happier dealing with animals than people, often used rather agricultural terms and I wondered how he would broach the subject when he met them that evening.

'Talking of mating,' he went on, 'haven't heard much about Gail recently. Has she now settled or what's going on in her world?'

Sir Charles was very good at keeping up to date with the comings and goings of most of his staff and quite a few of his tenants.

'I've slightly lost track at the moment but I'm afraid no, she hasn't really settled, well not as far as I know. Occasionally we have the usual hoohah

194

when some man's caused her some distress, or the other way round I'm never quite sure, but otherwise it's the usual rollercoaster I'm afraid, Sir Charles.'

'That girl would have been better out working the streets than being a farm secretary,' he announced rather harshly. I didn't really know how to reply which was probably just as well because at that moment there was a knock on the door and Gail came into the office.

'Oh, I'm sorry,' she said, 'I didn't realise you were here, Sir Charles. I'll come back later.'

'No, no, don't worry, Gail, I'm just leaving. I hope you are well,' he enquired.

'I'm very well, thank you, Sir Charles, but, really, I'll come back later.'

Despite his ageing years, Sir Charles had noticed the rather too short skirt, high heels and low-cut top that were Gail's trademark.

'See what I mean?' he commented as she left the room.

'Well I think she's very keen to find someone and settle down,' I said on her behalf. 'The problem is she thinks dressing like that attracts the men, which of course it does but it rather attracts the wrong sort of men. Not the sort that are likely to view her as a potential wife anyway.'

'Still we can't change her, and maybe one day she'll realise she's not going about this in the right way,' Sir Charles observed.

He then stood up to leave, saying, 'I'll let you know what Sebastian thinks once I've seen him this evening. Times moving on now, James, you know, I'm an old man and I'm starting to feel a little tired.'

I followed him out of the office, slightly alarmed by our brief meeting. I had never heard Sir Charles refer to himself as old or tired, and his moving out of the Hall would be a major change. I just hoped that Sebastian's and Serena's breeding programme was not imminent, as all of us would need time to adapt.

However, there were more immediate and pressing things to worry about, the most immediate being a visit to one of the tenant farmers, Jack White. He was a tenant farmer on the edge of the estate heading north towards Bury St Edmunds. I had an appointment to visit him at 10 am to discuss, as he put it, a revolutionary diversification that would enable him to pay his rent.

I always had a slight sense of foreboding when tenants rang to say they had got an idea which would help them pay the rent, because it usually meant they were after one of two things. Either they had come up with a harebrained scheme which needed landlord's approval, or they wanted a reduction in the rent.

Jack White was no different and I arrived at Tye Green Farm a few minutes late.

He came out to meet me.

'Good to see you, James,' he greeted me. 'I haven't seen you for a while, I must be behaving myself.'

He was about the same age as me and had taken on the tenancy from his father about two years earlier. His father, also called Jack, had been a traditional Suffolk farmer who had made a decent living out of growing cereal crops, sugar beet and a sizeable pig unit.

Jack Jr, as everyone called him, had continued the farming operations but had injected a new and more modern approach to his business. I found him a perfectly reasonable sort of fellow but he was not liked locally because of his cut-throat approach to business. He had managed to get vacant possession on two farmworkers' cottages by slightly devious means – he had moved the retired employees, into social housing in the village and then tarted up the houses in order to let them as holiday homes.

The estate had got drawn into it because he needed consent to let the cottages as such, they formed part of the farm tenancy, but I had had some sympathy with the view that the elderly tenants would be better off in the village. Indeed at first the tenants themselves had thought the idea sound as they could walk to the shops or the pub rather than be cut off living out in the sticks. From what I could make out though both the elderly couples who moved into the village found it quite difficult to adjust to having neighbours, streetlights and more noise, so the issue became clouded in controversy.

His latest venture turned out to be even more controversial.

We went into his office, which he had converted from one of the farm buildings. There were no dusty piles of invoices to be paid, stacks of Farmers Weekly, old boots and coats in there. It was a sleek manicured room with modern desks, computers and a steel glass-topped circular table at which we sat. Jack White Jr was a businessman and his business just so happened to be farming. In fact the only thing I noticed in his office that was at all reminiscent of a bygone era was his complimentary calendar hanging on the wall depicting attractive young ladies with no clothes on. Clearly some things would never change.

'James, would you like some coffee?' he asked, adding, 'How much time have you got?'

'I'd love some coffee, Jack,' I replied, 'and basically I've got as much time as we need.'

He went over to a very fancy-looking coffee machine and said, 'Excellent, because I really need to discuss this with you in some detail. What would you like, cappuccino, mocha or standard American?'

This was quite unlike most of the farms that I visited where we usually sat round the kitchen table and the most traditional of teapots, a large brown betty would be plonked down together with a plate of homemade shortbread.

'That's very sophisticated of you, Jack,' I said. 'I think I'll have a cappuccino then please.'

He twiddled a few knobs and there was a certain amount of gushing and hissing, followed by a small cloud of steam emanating from the machine and he brought back two cups of extravagant-looking coffee.

'Well, Jack,' I went on, 'this is certainly different from your father's day when we used to sit around the kitchen table and talk about the price of pigs.'

'James, you know as well as I do that times have moved on. Although mentioning pigs I have to admit that they are still a major income stream for the business. But no, you're quite right, things have moved on and I've been investigating various possibilities to increase the profit on this farm.'

'Everyone is looking for new revenue streams these days and knowing you, you'll be at the forefront of it.'

'This one is going to be fantastic if I can get it off the ground. But I've got a lot of hurdles to jump. The potential though is amazing but the two main bodies to get on board are the estate and the planners.'

'Tell me what you have in mind.'

'Before I tell you the details, James,' he went on, 'I have already had a meeting with the planners out here and in principle they are quite keen on it. I want to build a wind farm.'

I must have looked surprised because although I had expected some revolutionary idea, a wind farm hadn't crossed my mind.

'A wind farm – well that's certainly different.'

'Absolutely,' confirmed Jack, 'but it's definitely the way forward. All this talk about renewable energy and decreasing our reliance on fossil fuels, wind energy has got to be top of the agenda. And here, on this slight rise above the surrounding countryside is the ideal place in terms of wind velocities to site a wind farm. We've done some preliminary tests with one of the big energy people and they're keen to sign an option to take the development forward if I can get the consents.'

'Well, Jack, that is quite a proposal,' I agreed, 'and frankly I would be surprised if you could get the planning. I know the theory behind renewable energy is popular but no one wants to have a wind farm on their back doorstep.'

'No, I appreciate that,' he said, 'but I am keen to take it further.'

'I will speak to Sir Charles and the trustees about it but I have to warn you that my gut feeling is that they will not be that keen. Have you worked out the sort of income it might bring?'

'We have some approximate figures but it does all depend on the amount of electricity that's produced. I don't know whether you know much about this but basically it's to do with selling units of electricity generated by the turbines into the National Grid.'

'Yes, I've got some idea but I think if I take it to the trustees and Sir Charles you will have to give us an indication of the income and how much benefit there will be to the estate.'

He got up and went over to a computer and within a few minutes had printed off the proposal. The bottom line looked like it would produce about £30,000 a year for the estate. '

'Well, Jack, I'll take this and discuss it with Sir Charles first. It may well die there I have to warn you, but if not then it will go to the next trustees meeting.'

'James, thank you for that – any idea how long this might take?'

'Erm, I can see Sir Charles within the next week or so, and if it does go to a trustees meeting then we are talking about two to three months.'

'That's fine,' he said, 'I've got another meeting with the planners in six weeks time, so it should all fit in together.'

I drove away from his farm, reflecting on the changing face of rural estate management. Traditionally estate income had been earned mainly from rents, but more and more estates were diversifying and Jack White's idea was certainly one for the future.

With Sir Charles having mentioned only that morning that he was thinking about taking a back seat, I wondered whether Sebastian would take a more modern approach during his time as custodian of Frampton. It would be interesting to hear the outcome of Sir Charles' dinner with Sebastian and Serena in due course.

If that was the future I was abruptly brought back to the present, if not the past.

We still had two cottages in the village, and I hasten to add only two, that had outside WCs. I had tried all manner of ways of persuading the two respective tenants to let the estate install bathrooms, but had been met with blank refusal. This particular call had come from an elderly gentleman, the fiercely independent and stubborn Mr Jarvis who was certain that if he had an inside bathroom the rent would go up.

Mr Jarvis lived in a row of three tiny cottages in a back alley off the High Street and he appeared to do nothing more all day than sit in front of the television, which was turned to nearly full volume. His neighbours regularly complained, not only about the noise but also the dreadful state of his small back garden. But there was really nothing anyone could do about it as he was so set in his ways, cantankerous and difficult. I remembered going to visit him when the garden issue came up.

'I ain't gonna do anything with the garden. I like it like it is. I know why you're 'ere, Mr Aden, it's them bleedin' neighbours o' mine. All they want is a pretty little patch to look out on and I ain't got the strength to look after it, nor am I gonna pay anyone to do it for me.'

'I think we could get someone in to help you, Mr Jarvis,' I said. 'If it's not from the estate I'm sure we could get some sort of assistance from Social Services'.

'I'm not havin' those people in 'ere. Whenever I've had them 'ere they want this to change, and that to change, and I ain't gonna change anything. I've told you that.'

The cottage was in a sorry state and even the matter of painting the windows had become a drawn-out issue. Mr Jarvis hadn't wanted the inconvenience of a decorator, despite my insistence that the estate was duty bound to attend to the exterior. The place looked run down and so did Mr Jarvis when I went to see him about his WC.

I knocked on the door and a few flakes of paint fluttered off in the breeze. I could hear the television blasting away in the front room and so I was somewhat surprised when Mr Jarvis eventually opened the door.

'Ah, Mr Jarvis, I've come round to sort out this problem you've got. I'm surprised you heard me with that television on so loud.'

He peered at me. 'Oh, it's you, Mr Aden. Well I can tell you there's nothing wrong with my hearing.'

'Good, well perhaps you had better show me the problem.'

I took a deep breath and walked inside. It was one of those houses where I tried not to observe too closely or to breathe in too deeply. Fortunately we shuffled straight through into the back garden. Immediately outside the back door was a small yard with a brick-built shed dividing the yard from the garden beyond. The brick-built shed was the cause of my visit.

I really didn't want to go in there and prayed fervently that if Mr Jarvis opened the door I would be able to see the cause of the problem from afar.

'You told the office, Mr Jarvis, that there's a leak.'

'It's a bloody big leak too,' he said, 'like a bloody torrent.'

'Well, do you know where it's leaking from? Is it the water going in or going out? Can you be a bit more specific?'

'I can be bloody specific all right, Mr Aden,' he said. 'It's not the coming in or going out that's the problem, it's the bloody roof, look.' He pointed at the grey slates and there was a fairly sizeable gap which would have let a lot of rain run through.

'And it's just in the wrong place,' he went on, 'look, right above the pan it is, I can't go when its raining.'

I felt a wave of relief come over me as this matter could be dealt with from outside.

'Right, Mr Jarvis, I can see exactly what you mean and I'll get Tony to call round either this afternoon or tomorrow and repair it.'

He grunted and started shuffling back towards

the back door of the cottage.

'Of course there is still the option of putting a bathroom in the house for you, Mr Jarvis,' I ventured without much optimism.

He turned round slowly and stared at me.

'We've 'ad this discussion before,' he said, 'in fact we've 'ad it many times before and you know me thoughts. I'm 'appy as I am, Mr Aden, and I can't be doin' with any folk messin' about round here. It's bad enough with them damn neighbours either side of me always tryin' to poke their nose in. Don't like me telly on, want me garden sorted. Tell you what, Mr Aden, they'd rather see me dead and this place all tarted up.'

'Well I don't know about that,' I said, 'that's a bit harsh.'

'Bugger being harsh,' he said, 'that's the truth, but I'll tell you what, Mr Aden, I ain't about to die yet. I'm of the old school you know. A little bit of hardship never did anyone any harm.'

Clearly it hadn't affected his longevity but privately I wondered whether it had affected his outlook on life. There were all types of people in Frampton but I am quite sure that he was one of the most disagreeable.

I wondered fleetingly what Mr Jarvis might have to say over the proposal of a wind farm on the estate.

Chapter 16

Countryside activities, shows and fairs were usually colourful, lively and exciting. The annual ploughing match failed, in my view, to meet any of those descriptions. It was usually held in the autumn but due to the previous sodden October the event had been postponed. It took place in March on a field of stubble that the estate's home farm had kept for the occasion.

There must be some people who find the subject fascinating but watching paint dry appealed to me more.

Sir Charles, who usually did the prize-giving, was unwell and Sebastian and Serena were away, so the job fell to me. I had only once attended the ploughing match on the estate, usually managing to arrange a pressing engagement elsewhere.

With an official part to play I embraced it with more enthusiasm than otherwise I might have done. To be fair there was a lot more to ploughing than first met the eye. There were three categories: modern tractors, vintage tractors and horse-drawn. The eighty-acre field was divided up for the respective categories, and judges and marshals organised the competitors.

About half the field was reserved for modern tractors, and there was a surprising number of huge machines, particularly the distinctive green John Deere monsters, revving up and belching clouds of diesel fumes as they prepared for their turn. The aim in all classes appeared to be the straightness of the furrow and a uniform depth. The modern tractors with computerised hydraulics and earnest young men at the controls made a fine job of it and it was beyond me how the judges could really distinguish between the various efforts. They all looked beautifully cut and turned and the furrows ran into the distance in a line as straight as a die. There was good humour amongst the competitors, mainly young lads wearing boiler suits advertising various tractor manufacturers.

Next to their loud and busy activities were the vintage tractors. I recognised a few like the old grey Fergie, a Fordson Major and even an old David Brown Cropmaster.

The men, and I have to say men as I didn't see one woman driver, who operated these tractors were an entirely different breed. They tended to be late middle aged onwards and rather than plough for a living, did so out of an interest in working their machines. There were a lot of hearty guffaws and perhaps more camaraderie than competition. They favoured checked shirts, dungarees and a wild assortment of hats. Despite the considerably smaller size of their tractors the amount of bellowing smoke was in inverse proportion to their modern counterparts. The old tractors chugged up and down the field, clattering and heaving as they toiled against the heavy Suffolk clay.

Finally there were the few horse-drawn entries. These were the most interesting and it was a joy to see great carthorses like Shires and Percherons treading the ground. Of course in this area the Suffolk Punch was the most numerous and accounted for half the field. Seeing in front of me the evolution of farming mechanisation was quite shocking. Everybody knows how these things have changed but to watch 100 years of progress working on one field was a revelation. That was far more interesting than the straightness of the furrow.

The horsemen were yet again different from the tractor-men, and had a stoical patience as they set about their work. Clad in leather breeches and cloth caps they looked as though they were taking part in an adaptation of a Jane Austen novel.

Along the sidelines of all three categories were their followers and helpers. The modern men had their girlfriends playing about jesting at others' efforts, wearing jeans and tight-fitting sweatshirts announcing that YOUNG FARMERS LIKE TO DO IT.

The vintage tractor followers had probably once been like that but age and childbearing had put paid to both trim figures and energy. They fussed around Thermos flasks of tea and had a resigned air of acceptance of their husband's hobby.

The horse groupies were far too busy to do anything other than help their partners. Whether or not it was coincidence but the men behind the horse ploughs and their contingent seemed far leaner and fitter than any of those on the tractors. The horses needed brushing, plaiting, bits of brass polishing or leather to be soaped – altogether their activities were far more vigorous.

It was particularly interesting to reflect on how this change in mechanisation had altered the landscape in which we stood. The smaller fields that centuries ago had been ploughed by the horse had long disappeared. Hedges had been ripped out, ditches filled and vast expanses of open countryside might now consist of only two or three fields. This eighty-acre field was by no means the largest on the home farm, and yet 100 years ago eight acres might well have comprised a whole farm. I was reflecting on this when the organiser of the event, with the improbable but entirely appropriate name of Philip Ploughshare, tapped me on the shoulder.

I turned round.

'Ah, hello, Mr Ploughshare,' I said.

'It's about time, Mr Aden, I showed you what to do for the prize giving,' he told me. He was a large ruddy-faced jovial man, with no hair on his head. It all seemed to have been bunched together to form the most enormous eyebrows that I had ever seen. It was difficult to look the man straight in the eye, not because they overhung like an Old English sheepdog, but simply because of their extensive growth. The presence of a beard may have alleviated the phenomenon but Mr Ploughshare was clean-shaven.

'PP,' shouted a women in the distance, 'where do you want to put the table for the presentation?'

'I'll be over in a minute,' he shouted. 'I'm just talking to Mr Aden about it.'

'We'll have the table under that ash tree near the gate,' he advised me, 'it's where we always have it.'

'That's fine by me, I'm just here to do as you say really.'

'Well, it's really kind of you to come. I'm sorry that Sir Charles isn't well because he loves coming to this you know.'

'Yes, I know he does, and he sends his apologies. In fact it's not often that Sir Charles cancels anything so I have to say he can't be feeling very well at all.'

Philip Ploughshare, or PP as his wife called him, led me towards where he was intending to set up the table.

'As organiser,' I asked him, 'I imagine that you take part in these competitions?'

'Ooh, yes,' he said, 'I've been a plougher for about thirty years now. I've got a Fordson Major and I pull a Ransomes Single Furrow behind it,' he explained. 'But as secretary to the Frampton Ploughing Society I can't take part in this one.'

'No, I can see that – you've got your hands full running around after this lot.'

'I have that.' He laughed. 'And you have to watch these tykes or we get in a terrible muddle.'

As we talked, Mr Ploughshare started to unload a couple of trestle tables from the back of his van. Mrs PP was ably assisting him and produced a long white linen tablecloth, which she draped over the tables and held down with metal clips around the edges. The tables were a little unsteady, being upon stubble ground, and I helped find some pieces of flint to try to steady them.

Mrs PP set about arranging the considerable number of trophies. They ranged from a large silver cup, which must have been about eighteen inches high, to some smaller silver trophies, a ceramic model of a Shire horse, several bottles of whisky and a hardbacked book about flower arranging.

I asked what all these things were for. There seemed to be more trophies than there were competitors and a rather odd selection of what I assumed were prizes.

'Well, you'll recognise that large silver trophy, that's the Frampton trophy for the overall winner of the championship. This one is for the straightest furrow by a pair of horses, this one is for a tractor pre-1950, this one is for tractors over 150 horse power...' and so it went on. It seemed as though you could win a trophy for ploughing with nearly anything.

'They've all been donated by people over the years,' he went on to explain, 'and that's why we are fortunate to have so many. And people give us prizes as well, usually bottles as you can see.'

I also saw the book on flower arranging but was unable to grasp the connection between whoever won that and their ploughing skills.

Time was getting on now and I was now a little chilly. My earlier cultivated enthusiasm for regarding this activity with some interest had waned. The ploughing had all finished but dozens of people were walking up and down the field poking at the furrows.

'How long does this go on?' I asked, indicating the general activity on the field.

'Oh, they'll be done in the next twenty minutes or so,' I was assured. 'They're just having a good look at the furrows.'

I had a good look at my watch. Mrs PP must have seen me because she came bustling over and asked if I would like a cup of tea.

I looked enviously at the bottles of whisky on display, even a fine single malt or two amongst them, but there was no suggestion of unscrewing their caps. Instead, Mrs PP walked over to the car and rummaged about in the boot. She brought back a blue plastic beaker, three quarters full, of deliciously strong but tepid tea. I hadn't asked for sugar but there was a generous helping in it.

I thanked her and took a sip. It was quite revolting. I certainly didn't want to drink it but with just the three of us standing around the presentation table I was unable to pour it away. So I pretended to take a few mouthfuls and then, with what I hoped was a convincing degree-of drama, dropped the cup. My actions were made to look all the more sincere because, instead of the thing landing on the grass where I had intended, it hit the table and spilt all over the white linen tablecloth.

'Oh, my goodness, Mrs Ploughshare,' I said with genuine apology. 'I am so sorry, I'm not sure what happened.'

'Oh, it doesn't matter,' she said graciously, although I could see from the expression on her face that it did indeed matter, it mattered considerably.

I felt very awkward. After all, although the outcome was a mistake, I had poured tea over the white, carefully ironed, linen tablecloth. It was also obvious that there wasn't a spare. To make matters worse the stain spread rapidly across nearly half of one of the tables. The china Shire horse looked as though it had urinated.

'I will rush up to the Hall and see if I can find a replacement,' I suggested.

'No, no, don't worry, Mr Aden,' she said, 'there isn't time. Look, they're beginning to come over for the prize-giving. We'll just have to put up with it, so don't worry. Anyway, let me go and get you another cup of tea.'

'Oh, no, please don't do that,' I assured her, 'it's really not necessary.'

'No, I will,' she said, halfway back to the car, 'there's plenty left in the Thermos.'

This seemed doubly unfair. Not only had I ruined the cloth but I was now going to have to face another cup of horrible tea. Within a minute I was back in the same predicament. I took a sip or two and waited anxiously for the competitors to assemble around our sorry-looking presentation table, willing them to gather so that I could put the beaker down on the grass this time. Amidst the bustle of cheery-faced ploughmen I deftly gave the cup a tap with my left boot and it toppled over harmlessly, emptying the tea into the stubble.

'Ladies and gentlemen,' shouted Mr Plough-share, 'welcome to the annual Frampton plough-ing match and here to present the prizes is the Frampton Estate manager, Mr James Aden.'

There was a murmur of applause and I took my position.

'Thank you, Philip,' I said. 'Ladies and gentle-men, Sir Charles sends his apologies as he is unwell and cannot attend today. You will probably all know how much he enjoys the ploughing match and I can assure you that if he could he would have been here to present the prizes. So he has asked me to stand in for him and I must thank you for having me here. I have had an extremely interesting day seeing you all at work with your various ploughs. So, let's get on with the prize-giving.'

Philip Ploughshare then passed me the trophies in turn, telling me what they were for. It took some time and I think everybody present must have received some award or other for recognition of their efforts during the day. Nobody mentioned the stained tablecloth and the beaming ruddy faces expressed delight at a wonderful day out.

Two weeks later, Sophie and I had our own day out watching something much faster and potentially more dangerous than ploughing. We had been invited to the Suffolk Hunt point to point. Our host was a neighbouring farmer to Cordwainers, Clarence Haughley-Sprout. He described himself as a farmer, and indeed he lived on a farm of sorts. The house was a massive Victorian pile, maintained in a state of extreme neglect, together with about 100 acres. The 100 acres were used to exemplify the cutting edge of progressive farming, as Clarence put it. Everything he did was to extreme. His house didn't just need a bit of updating, it was about to fall down. His avant-garde farming ventures ranged, depending on the latest article he had read in the newspaper, from ostriches to chinchillas, worms to edible snails. He was currently experimenting with alpacas, which spent as much time in our fields as his, due to a new type of electric fence that he had installed. It was powered by wind and only appeared to work during a howling gale.

Clarence Haughley-Sprout was an impeccable host and even from across the members' car park it was clear upon our arrival that he had already assembled quite a gathering around his car. He drove a 1940s Lagonda, which was better preserved than his house and probably worth more. It was a beautiful car with great sweeping running boards, chrome headlights the size of meat platters and highly polished spoke wheels. Clarence's income wasn't a result of his farming activities and as he never appeared to engage in any other form of activity his means remained a mystery.

His larger-than-life character was complemented by his attire. His massive breeches, tweed cape, bow tie and deerstalker emphasised his stature.

As soon as he saw us, he shouted, 'James and Sophie, my dears, how delightful to see you both. My dearest neighbours in the world,' he announced to all those around him. And, I thought, everyone else in the members' car park.

'Come over and meet these people,' he went on, 'all my lovely friends, I expect you know some of them. Come now Sophie, what will you have to drink?'

He opened the boot of his Lagonda which contained a highly polished mahogany drinks cabinet, especially commissioned for the car.

'Gin and tonic, m'dear, that's your tipple isn't it?'

Without waiting for an answer he picked up a

cut-glass tumbler, opened one little drawer and procured some ice cubes, another revealed a pair of exquisite silver tongs and slices of fresh lemon, which were deftly placed in the tumbler to which equal amounts of gin and tonic were added.

Clarence had the ability to consume vast quantities of alcohol without it having any noticeable effect. For his guests though it was a different matter, and one or two of his guests already had the slight sway of someone who has drunk too much on an empty stomach.

'Tuck into that,' he advised Sophie, practically engulfing her in his cape as he put his arm around her in greeting.

'And James, you'll have a whisky and soda as usual.' It wasn't really a question, more of a statement because in Clarence's view all men drank whisky and soda, whether they liked it or not.

Another crystal tumbler was located and he opened and closed the little mahogany drawers procuring more ice and this time a silver cocktail stick, with which he stirred my drink.

'A couple of these, James,' he announced to all those gathered, 'and you'll be picking a few winners, mark my words.'

I thought rather than pick a few winners it was highly likely to impair any vague judgement that I might have had with racehorses. Clarence's parties always went the same way and I was thankful that we had left Emma with Mrs Painter at Cordwainers, and that I had arranged a taxi to collect us after the last race.

'We'll have a couple before the first race,'

Clarence told us, 'and then a bit of lunch.'

By the time we got to lunch both Sophie and I were a little giggly and, come to that, so were most of the party. Only Clarence remained as clear-headed as he had been from the start.

With some assistance he then organised the arrangement of the picnic table. It was a trestle-type affair similar to the one used at the ploughing match, but on this occasion the white linen cloth was unblemished and instead of trophies and prizes the table was soon laid with bone china, silverware and crystal.

Fortunately it wasn't raining, although the day was cold with a slight chill in the east wind.

I think there were twelve guests but I have to admit to rather a hazy recollection of what we ate. I do remember being impressed by the champagne coolers being continually replenished with fresh bottles. Smoked salmon, quails eggs, and little things covered with caviar swim amongst my recollections but as always with Clarence, the event degenerated into an alcoholic haze.

I believe that either Sophie or I won some money on the horses because we returned home with more cash in our wallets than when we set out.

Point to points were special in our memories. Our first date when Sophie was a student at Rumshott Estate and I was Deputy Agent had been at a point to point.

Chapter 17

When I had been working for Earl Leghorn at Rumshott, his son, Viscount Rumshott, had asked me to visit an estate in the Scottish Highlands, which he subsequently bought and Sophie and I then went to manage. It was during that first visit that Sophie and I became engaged and although our factorship in the Highlands was short-lived due to Sophie's uncle dying and leaving us Cordwainers Hall, we liked to return when we could.

It was fortunate for us that amongst Sir Charles' considerable property he owned the Strathard Estate, just north of Inverness. It was only about thirty miles as the crow flies from the Glen Arrin Estate where we had initially gone as a newly married couple.

Sir Charles' estate was smaller than Glen Arrin although it still extended to about 40,000 acres. It had all the ingredients of a magical Highland sporting estate and I grasped every opportunity I could to visit. We made sure that Sophie was always free at the time and would make the long journey north together, not only to reminisce but also to explore new areas of the estate.

Sir Charles had a factor running the estate, which he did supremely well. But as the Frampton Hall Estate was the senior estate I had a sort of overall head agent role, which encompassed overseeing the management of the Scottish land. To an extent that seemed unfair as the Scottish factor, Angus McKay, did a superb job and certainly did not need my interference. The key point was, however, that Strathard made a thumping loss in financial terms and had to be subsidised by Frampton.

Sporting estates in the highlands always have been and always will be a rich man's plaything. Occasionally one sees some laird try to make a go of it by opening the castle to shooting guests, or perhaps selling time-share fishing on his rivers, but by and large it is better to forget all that and accept that the thing will cost money. And lots of it.

Sophie and I had gone up to Scotland early in December, ostensibly for me to review the financial situation with Angus McKay, but in reality to enjoy five days of messing about on the hills. Fishing was over and there was a small amount of hind stalking. There was also, rather bizarrely, a pheasant shoot.

'It's a bit of a wee experiment,' explained Mr McKay. Angus McKay was considerably older than myself and we had settled at an early stage on a formal relationship. 'I asked Sir Charles about it and he seemed keen to give it a try,' he continued, 'and the fact of the matter is, Mr Aden, it's turned out quite well.'

'Well, it does seem rather surprising to have a pheasant shoot up in this rather bleak landscape,' I agreed. 'Who came up with the idea?'

'Well, I have to say it was my idea, but Sir Charles thought it an interesting experiment.'

I wondered who benefited the most from the experiment in that Sir Charles tended to fish and, in his advancing years, occasionally stalk when he was resident on the estate. However, my question was soon answered.

'Sir Charles considered it a bit of a perk for me, I think,' said Mr McKay, 'as he's only ever once been out since we started.'

Well that explained it and it was no surprise that Sir Charles had agreed to such an idea. He was always a most considerate employer. Some owners wanted every last drop of blood from employees and tenants alike, and inevitably their estates were populated by resentful and antagonistic people. Sir Charles' example of patronage kept his flock around him and ultimately, not only were his estates happier places to live, but the enthusiasm and generosity worked both ways.

In the event, during our five-day visit, we were invited to take part in this experimental pheasant shoot. Sophie was not keen on shooting but was quite happy to beat, and as we had left Emma at home with Mrs Painter she had some time to herself.

At the duly appointed hour we assembled in an estate farmyard. It was a dry and sunny day but the northeasterly wind was bitingly cold. Angus McKay had explained that both the keeper and beaters were local part-timers who helped him and warned us that it was a low-key, informal affair. The keeper, who I gathered was a fitter on the oil rigs at Invergordon, was a huge man. Jock McPherson had arms the size of a semi-mature pine tree and legs with the circumference of a mature oak. With a bald head and a grotesquely untamed grey beard I suspected that he could frighten all the birds out of a wood without the help of any beaters. Sophie was summoned none-theless to join his party.

The rest of his party comprised a few wiry Scotsmen, some leathery-faced women and many children. They all took delight in thwacking short sticks against their weatherproof trousers in the manner of an orchestra warming up before the curtain is raised.

This savage-looking line of beaters also had the accompaniment of as many dogs. The keeper appeared to favour large, stout black Labradors but there were nearly as many spaniels, a couple of terriers and even a dog that appeared to have escaped from an African township.

The guns were also of various types. Angus McKay and myself were in estate tweeds, as was one other chap. The other three guns – there were only six of us – included a farmer type in waxed Barbour, a man who looked like he was a member of the Ramblers Association wearing a cagoule and a friend of Jock's who was wearing a boiler suit, Wellington boots and a deerstalker.

We all introduced ourselves in the yard and had a glass of sloe gin before we set off. The beaters had the luxury of a tractor and trailer and were carted off into the distance, whilst the guns walked down some tracks to the first drive.

Angus positioned us on our pegs and we waited with great anticipation, hearing the hollers and shouting in front of us as the beaters crashed-through a strip of maize. All sorts of birds were flying out of it but they were rather small and definitely not on our list of targets.

Just as the beaters reached the end of the maize, having found no game birds at all, a strong cock pheasant squawked madly and took to the air. The wretched thing launched himself directly in my range. I was totally unprepared for the moment, as indeed were the rest of the guns, the beaters, and anyone else who happened to be within sight. I fired both barrels but it flew on undisturbed without so much as a flick of the tail to acknowledge my effort.

It was clear that the assembled party thought nothing of my effort either. The stunned motionless gaze that fell upon me was worse than any shouts of criticism. My formal tweed attire of plus fours and extremely wide matching cap made me feel worse. If I had been dressed in a boiler suit and builder's boots perhaps no one would have expected much of me.

Matters degenerated further on the second drive when the chap who was dressed in the boiler suit had the hot spot. Hot spot being a relative term in that four out of the five birds that appeared on the drive flew over him, but he killed them cleanly on the first shot every time.

By now the northeasterly wind was more than uncomfortable, it was causing pain. I almost feared a bird flying within my range, as I would need to lift my arms and lose what little warmth was left in me. At the end of the fourth drive a break for hot soup was promised and by then the party had bagged eight pheasants, a pigeon and another bird of unknown identity. Fortunately I hadn't shot it but there was a general consensus amongst the group that it might have been of a rare species. If so, it was rarer now.

We returned to the farmyard for our break and the farmhouse beckoned. No doubt roaring fires would have been lit and the central heating full on to ward away the evil effects of the wind. The Scots were clearly more robust than I because they made no move towards the house. Instead we stood around the back of an old Land Rover in the yard and in such a position that the wind funnelled into our meeting place.

The tinned hot tomato soup was the best I have ever tasted. Mind you, by then a cup of warm dog's pee would have been a delight. I could hardly believe that the man with the boiler suit was not wearing a coat and worse still had no gloves.

I asked him about it. 'Aren't you freezing cold?'

'Och, nay,' he replied, 'there's a bit of a wind I grant thee, but it's nay what I'd call a really cold day.'

He must have noticed me shivering, and the noise of my teeth banging against each other probably gave him an indication that I didn't share his view.

'If you wanna feel the cold,' he went on, 'you wanna come out on the rigs in the North Sea in January.'

That was an invitation I could refuse.

Abruptly we set off for the next four drives, which was to be the sum total for the day. The shoot was organised to end at about 2 pm, followed by lunch in a hotel nearby.

We marched out again refreshed by the soup. Sophie and the other beaters were in good spirits because their active running around the woods and coverts kept them warm, likewise the sturdy Highlanders who marched forth to their positions as though it were a mild spring day. I marched in a similar fashion to that of a penguin crossing the South Polar ice cap, the man in the boiler suit remarking, 'You're still a wee bit cold there by the look of ye I should have thought that wee bit of soup had warmed ye through.'

'It did help a bit,' I agreed, 'but I'm afraid I always do feel the cold and to my mind it is bloody perishing up here.'

He laughed as though I had made a joke but I suspected he was revelling in the discomfort of a wee namby Englishman with thoughts of avenging Culloden on his mind.

'Och, well,' he reassured me, 'the wind's bound to drop soon, I've no doubt.'

He clearly was not a proficient weather forecaster because shortly after he uttered those words it began to snow.

Well, this was great. Not only had it started to snow but Angus McKay, walking alongside me, told me that on the drive I would be in the hot spot and could expect the best shooting of the day. I was so bitterly cold that I almost feigned an illness, not just a mild cold but something altogether more serious. But somehow, as one does, I forced myself on in the name of good manners.

I was shown to my peg and it was with some relief I saw that it had been positioned in a slight

223

hollow out of the worst of the wind. A sickly looking hawthorn bush added some extra break from the wind, which was far more than the previous drives where the only shelter available had been a short bamboo cane stuck into the ground.

As Angus McKay had predicted I was standing in the hot spot for the drive. After waiting in silence for at least twenty minutes I then heard the shouts of the beaters some distance away. Gradually the tapping and cries of 'get up there', 'go on', and commands to the dogs crept closer and suddenly both pheasants appeared at the same time flying straight over me.

Much to my relief, and some amazement, I took a clean left and right and killed them outright. This was a considerable boost to my morale and at last created a favourable impression on the rest of the party.

There followed three more drives and although a few birds appeared they wisely flew back over the beaters and away from the guns. The only other thing that flew overhead was an RAF Tornado. Apart from being an embarrassing entry into one's game book, it was out of range for most of the guns.

I mentioned this in jest to Angus McKay as we finished the shoot, who I think was a little disappointed, if not despondent about the size of the bag.

'Aye,' he remarked drily, 'but I reckon the cost of these birds isn't far off the cost of that plane.'

Despite the fact that he had warned us that his shoot was only an experiment and we were not to expect much, it was clear that he must have put a great deal of energy and his own money into trying to make something of it. The evidence was now plain as to why there are few pheasant shoots on the high ground in the Scottish Highlands.

Nonetheless, Sophie and I had enjoyed the day. When I say that I had enjoyed the day I really mean in the sense that it was over. There is something invigorating and wholesome about spending the waking hours frozen to the bone amongst rugged and beautiful scenery that makes you feel good. It doesn't seem like it at the time but once we had retired to the Lovat Arms in Beauly the world seemed a happier place.

The hotel had set up a long rectangular table for us and we enjoyed a hearty meal with wine and whisky. Fortunately neither Sophie nor I were driving, as the unfamiliar mix of wine and whisky was a certain recipe for getting quickly drunk with a horrendous hangover to follow the day after. At least that's what happened to us and it was fortunate that we didn't have to get up early.

The next morning, staying in a guest bedroom at Sir Charles' lodge, we had a cooked breakfast and a day to ourselves walking on the estate. The joy of these occasional visits to Strathard was that we always allowed enough time to make the visit part work and part relaxation. We were free to walk on the hills wherever we wanted as there was no hind stalking taking place and chose a recommended route that took us along a small gently rising incline, a devilishly demanding climb and then a drop down into a wide and remote glen on the other side.

Sophie was equipped with the latest Gore-Tex equipment but despite her suggestions that I should invest in something similar I still preferred my tweeds. As we climbed over the steep ascent I was beginning to wish that I had taken her advice. My heavy tweed coat was far too hot and cumbersome and I would have carried it except for the rain. I struggled to keep up with her but kept reminding myself that once we were over the top my tweeds would come into their own. Indeed they did.

The breeze that had been gentle as we made our way up the first glen transformed into the biting northeasterly from which I had suffered the previous day. This time being on the move the cold was merely a presence rather than a pain. The tweed kept me warm and dry and once the worst of the climb was over I felt exhilarated to be in such a wild unspoilt landscape.

We followed a small path created by the deer that roamed the glen, alongside a small stream tumbling over rocks. The river was no more than ten feet across and only one or two feet deep. Occasionally the path would cross it and we would carefully pick our way using rocks as stepping stones to avoid soaking our boots. There were few deer in the glen but many way up on the hills and we would occasionally spot them. At one point we heard the shrieking cry of an eagle and stopped to listen. In fact there were a pair of golden eagles and through our pocket binoculars we spent a while observing them circling in huge sweeps across one of the hillsides. Gradually though they soared higher and higher until even through the binoculars they were mere specks in the sky. It was a sign of the solitude and wildness of the Highlands that was so endearing to both of us.

By the time we got back to the lodge we were both exhausted but with a sense of well being. Mrs McLeod the housekeeper had a roaring log fire going in the library and she brought in tea and shortbread. Being Sir Charles' establishment the tea was in a Georgian silver teapot and the cups and saucers were of some antique bone china that had probably been in the lodge for the past 100 years. Little plates with homemade shortbread and white linen napkins were a further touch to show that this was one of the grand sporting lodges in the Highlands and how fortunate we were to be guests.

After tea we took baths in copious amounts of steaming hot water. The bathtubs were the size of children's swimming pools, constructed of cast iron with ball-and-claw feet and taps the size of something from a cruise liner's engine room.

Sir Charles insisted on a dress code at dinner even if he wasn't in residence. He had dispensed with black tie and long dresses, but jacket and tie and dresses were still expected. We duly changed and went down to the drawing room for an aperitif before dinner.

The drawing room at Strathard Lodge was, as one would expect, formal and very Scottish. It had a superb tartan carpet and dozens of stags' heads were mounted on the walls. Each one had the initials of who had shot it, when and where. Although it was a large room there was a selection of sofas and chairs near the open fire, which gave it an intimate and cosy feel.

It had been arranged by some sort of invitation, and although I am not sure whether we invited them or whether they invited themselves, Angus McKay and his wife joined us for dinner.

It was a slightly odd formality in that both he and I were Sir Charles' land agents so, as it were, of equal standing, and yet Sophie and I were entertaining them in Sir Charles' house and at Sir Charles' expense.

Angus' wife, whom we had not met before, was of rather an unexpected nature. I suppose we were expecting a rather dour Scotswoman as might befit a factor's wife in the Scottish Highlands but Shirley, as she insisted we call her despite the maintained professional formalities of her husband, originated from the Black Country just outside Birmingham. She was large to the point of plumpness with skin that looked as soft as a peach and was as outgoing and loud as a stand-up comedienne.

The awesome difference between the pair of them was a shock. It was almost as shocking as her language, which was certainly near the bone, and she had retained her Black Country accent. It seemed totally incongruous in the rather grand setting of a highland lodge and formal dinner.

Fortunately, Mrs McLeod had arranged the meal in the smaller of the two dining rooms and she was the only member of staff present. It did calm the sense of formality a little but not quite enough to dispel the sense of unreality that the evening presented.

Inevitably at some time during the evening we asked how they had met and Angus, who began some long complicated explanation, was interrupted by his wife.

'Well,' said Shirley, 'it was all a bit naughty at the start, weren't it, Angus? I was up in Scotland on a course for the firm that I worked for at the time, and I saw Angus in the hotel bar where we were staying.'

Angus shifted uncomfortably in his chair and I suspected he must have heard this dozens of times before.

'Anyway, you know what it's like at these company things and I'd had a bit to drink. The girls at my table challenged me to chat up a Scotsman in a kilt. You know there was a bottle of vodka on it, so I went up to him and I said to him, "Excuse me, Mister Scotsman, but the girls and I," and I pointed over at my friends, "want to know whether there's anything worn under your kilt?"'

Angus butted in, 'They nay want to hear all about this ridiculous tale,' he said.

'Oh, I think they do,' she replied. 'Anyway,' she continued without hesitation, 'the old joke is that he should have said, "No, madam, as far as I know everything is in good working order." But he didn't.' She laughed and said, 'He said, would you believe it, "Why don't you find out?"'

Angus, who was taking a slug of wine, almost choked. 'I'm sure I did nae say that.'

'Oh, but you did, Angus, 'cos I can remember telling the girls and they all thought that was a far funnier reply than the one you should have made.'

Sophie and I were captivated by this extraordinary tale, mostly because it seemed so incongruous as to be believable. Fortunately everyone had had a few glasses of wine by this time so it was all very funny, but I vaguely wondered how Angus would deal with the situation when I saw him the next day.

True to form he acted as though nothing had been said and we maintained our formal professional relationship as if the conversation had never taken place.

At lunchtime the following day, Sophie and I had to catch the plane back to England and Angus kindly drove us to Inverness airport. The business matters of the estate had been dealt with for the time being and we had enjoyed our couple of days relaxing in the Highlands. We always felt some regret at leaving Scotland and even in our happy, contented lives in Suffolk there was the occasional yearning to be back in the wild remoteness of the glens.

Chapter 18

We got back from Scotland and I was immediately plunged into a Frampton dilemma.

Colonel John Biggin, the tenant of a rather attractive Georgian farmhouse on the estate, came to see me. Due to his advancing years he wanted to move from the house into the village. He was a bachelor in his late seventies and a somewhat distant cousin to Sir Charles. As a relative he had originally been granted a lifelong tenancy of the house but clearly the cost of managing the house and its gardens was becoming too much.

'I've decided,' he barked, sitting in my office, 'that I'd like to move into the village from White House, and find something more suitable for a man of my years.'

In a sense this was good news because the colonel rented White House for a minuscule amount that had been set some twenty years previously. If it was available to refurnish and re-let, financially the estate would be better off. But the colonel was quite demanding in the type of cottage that he would require in place of White House.

'Don't take me as a fool, young man,' he said as though he was commanding a subaltern in his regiment. 'I realise that if I give up the tenancy on my house then there's a benefit to the estate, so I need to have a reasonable cottage in the village to suit my requirements.'

'I do realise, Colonel, that we could re-let the White House to considerable advantage in the present day, so let me know what you want and I'll see if we can find a cottage that's suitable for you in the village.'

'It's not that I'm infirm or can't cope with it, you know,' he carried on, 'but I think village life might be quite enjoyable for a man of my age.'

'I'm sure it would. There's a lot going on here, especially in the evenings and it's likely that rather than being stuck out in the sticks you could enjoy some of Frampton's nightlife,' I said with some jest.

However, he was not of a jovial kind and merely continued, 'So, Aden, I need a house with three bedrooms, a couple of reception rooms and a reasonable garden.'

I couldn't quite imagine why he needed three bedrooms because as a lifelong bachelor he had no family and would only need room for the occasional guest to stay.

'And a bit of privacy,' he continued. 'I need a house where I can go out and pee on the lawn.'

I knew what he meant but finding a house in the village that met such exact criteria would be difficult. As a rule we tried not to have empty houses as it did not make financial sense although with such a number of them there was always a certain amount of changeover.

'Do you think you can find me something, Aden?' he asked. 'I'm not in a hurry but now I've made up my mind I'd like to get on with it.'

He was the archetype of a retired colonel. Tall and lean, with thinning white hair and a handle-bar moustache. I imagined he would have been quite foreboding in his army days. Now, with advancing years, he was slightly stooped and arthritic. But he still addressed everyone as though they were his troops and expected them to take notice of his commands. The fact that he was a friend of and distantly related to Sir Charles made him even more authoritarian. It was going to be difficult to find him a house that not only suited his demands but that he would see as appropriate for his position.

At our next management meeting I spoke to Sir Charles about it.

'I suppose the Colonel has already mentioned that he'd like to give up White House and move into the village?' I asked.

'Oh, yes, he did mention that,' agreed Sir Charles. 'Mind you it was some time ago. Since then it had all gone quiet and I thought he had dropped the idea. Frankly I can't imagine him living in a village cottage.'

'Nor can I, Sir Charles, but he does seem quite keen on "downsizing", as people like to put it.'

'Well, he's a funny old boy,' continued the baronet. 'As you know he is a sort of relative and he's a good pal of mine actually but I have to say I think he's a bit, um, you know, full of his own self-importance. He's never really got over leaving the army.'

'Well I suppose he does rather behave as though he's still in the army, Sir Charles. We tend to get orders rather than requests.' I laughed.

'I always find it strange,' continued Sir Charles, 'that he never got further than a colonel. I mean he's devoted his whole life to the army and I believe he was a very good soldier, but when you think about it for a while, you would have thought he would have gone a bit further, at least to brigadier.'

'Well, possibly,' I agreed, 'but I don't really know the Colonel socially so I'm not sure what to say.'

'No, no, I'm sure not. Anyway it's nothing to do with you and finding him a house. No doubt he'll be on at me again so have a think and see what might be coming up and let me know. We can go from there.'

We left it at that for the time being and there wasn't much else I could do about it. Apart from the occasional terraced cottage, nothing became available during the following couple of months.

The first inkling that I had about a suitable house came, not unsurprisingly, through Gail. In fact it was not only through Gail but because of Gail that the situation arose.

Anne, who knew most of the goings on in the village although maintained a discreet silence, also knew most of the matters that I was dealing with at any time. She came into my office one morning.

'I think, James,' she said, 'that there could be a suitable house for the colonel before long.'

'Is there?' I asked. 'Which house and what makes you say that?'

'Well, you know I don't like to meddle in village gossip,' she continued, 'but there's been another incident, if I may put it that way, to do with Gail.'

I must have looked somewhat resigned as these 'incidents' that Gail embroiled herself in on a regular basis inevitably ended up becoming part of the life of the office.

'Anne,' I continued, 'I dread to think what you are going to tell me. In fact I don't want to hear. If that woman throws us into yet another tawdry affair then not only is she leaving this office but she'll have to leave the village.'

Anne looked slightly shocked and although I knew she wasn't a close friend of Gail, I think she had some sympathy for her colleague's dilemma.

We were particularly busy at the time on the estate, not only because matters were progressing slightly in the proposed take-over by Sebastian, but also because I was carrying out a revaluation of the assets. We also had a number of rent reviews due and major repair work going on at the Hall. Plus, I was busy at Cordwainers with Sophie and the farm. Gail would be the straw that broke the camel's back.

But as it happened, Gail did prove to be the answer to the colonel's request. The sordid details behind what happened eventually became public knowledge but at the time I was fortuately only provided with sketchy facts.

The estate owned a lovely Georgian-fronted house on the High Street which looked suitably grand from outside but in fact only contained two reception rooms and four bedrooms, which I suppose is generally considered quite a substantial house.

It had been rented for a long time by a couple

who were well known and liked in the village despite their unorthodox arrangement, at least in terms of Frampton society. Jeremy Wood, an extremely agreeable and effervescent artist in his late fifties, and his companion with the unusual name of Isaac Sunflower, some twenty years younger, lived in apparent harmony. That was until Gail intruded on their domestic bliss.

Isaac, who didn't seem to have a job at all, had apparently met Gail at the yoga classes in the village hall. It was a surprise to me that Gail attended yoga classes for two reasons. Firstly, she didn't appear to have the kind of physique that would lend itself to any yoga positions and secondly, it was frequented solely by women. Except Isaac Sunflower, who was considered by many to be an honorary woman.

I am not familiar with the theories behind yoga but I believe they do something to bring out the inner self in you. Evidently they brought out the inner self in Isaac and his allegiance turned, not only from one gender to another, but from the devastated Mr Wood to Gail.

The whole episode was made worse because Mr Wood was quite a well-known painter and when news of the scandal broke it was splashed across various tabloid newspapers, thrusting Gail into the limelight yet again. There was also a lot of thrusting by Mr Sunflower according to the articles in the papers.

The devastation brought upon Mr Wood was such that he decided to retire to his London flat and Isaac, with no means to support himself, moved into Gail's cottage. The house was surrendered back to the estate and I was able to offer it to the colonel.

Initially, I thought the problem was solved but the colonel was an old-fashioned man with old-fashioned principles and the first mention I made of it to him was not encouraging.

'That's that place where those two poofs lived,' he said in outrage. 'I'm not bloody well going in there. I'll catch all sorts of diseases, I've no doubt. Dammed disgusting behaviour. I'll be tarnished with the same brush.'

I could not really see that he would be tarnished with the same brush, as he put it, or how he could catch any sort of disease. In fact I wondered what sort of disease he was referring to as both Mr Wood and Mr Sunflower were in remarkably good health, at least until the scandal broke.

'Colonel,' I said, 'it's up to you. But it's the only suitable house that the estate is likely to have for the foreseeable future so I suggest you at least come and have a look at it. And, I might add, it has the most wonderful, totally private, walled garden. So if you insist on peeing on the lawn it will suit you admirably.'

It must have been the presence of a walled garden that changed his view because the following day he rang back.

'Aden,' he barked, 'I'll have a look at the house, 2 pm this afternoon, if you don't mind.'

He was commanding his soldiers again but fortunately the time suited. He still believed that he was doing the estate a great favour by giving up White House and moving into the village, and

237

although it was probably better for the village, and certainly for me, if he stayed well out of it, Sir Charles had agreed to help him.

At 1.55 pm, the colonel arrived at the estate office. He commanded Anne to show him into my office, which she did with a sense of trepidation as he tended to instil nervousness into those he considered his subordinates.

'Aden, you got the keys? We'll go and look at this poofs' parlour – see what we can do about it.'

I didn't feel there was a suitable response to that so I spoke to Anne.

'Have you got the keys to the Shirtmakers House?' I asked her. 'I'll take the colonel to have a look around.' In the late nineteenth century the house and workshop had been lived in by the village shirtmaker. Colloquially, since the occupation of Messrs Wood and Sunflower it had been renamed something similar but either the colonel never knew that or he did not understand the connection.

Whatever it was called, I took the colonel to see it. To my surprise he was enamoured by the place. Inevitably, artistic people of whatever gender tend to have an eye for interior design and the house was beautifully decorated and had been maintained to an immaculate standard. Furthermore, the walled garden was a delight beyond any expectation, and the colonel, who was a difficult man to please, fell in love with it immediately.

All this property business seemed so simple compared to the personnel issues I was having. I only had a few staff to look after but the disruption they could cause was disproportionate to the rest of the estate business.

When Gail had settled, in the past, albeit briefly, with a new acquaintance our lives generally became quieter. With this high-profile case involving a famous artist and a chap batting for the other side it was unclear whether she would settle into contented bliss or a long convoluted drama. With typical melodramatics she started to arrive at work wearing large sunglasses and a hat, in the fashion of a film star not wanting to be photographed by the paparazzi. She had managed to get her picture plastered over the tabloids and become a local celebrity, which she rather enjoyed. Anne and Brenda, who had in the past taken a somewhat motherly attitude towards her, took a step back as it seemed to have given Gail a new confidence. But once all the excitement had died down and she returned to her normal life we expected the worst – the sale of her story to the national press.

In a sense I dreaded the comedown. I feared that any attempt to further her recognition with torrid accounts of how she managed to convert her new-found friend with the buxom clasp of her sensuous personality would end in disaster.

To my relief, and quite possibly all of those in Frampton, these developments did not occur. At least for the foreseeable future, Gail appeared content and her domestic arrangements would remain behind closed doors.

Having the domestic matters of both the colonel and Gail settled, all that was left to complete the triangle was the re-letting of White House. For years the colonel had rented it at a minuscule rent due to Sir Charles' vaguely philanthropic views towards his distant cousin. Now was the chance to let it on reasonable terms and increase estate income.

Although Sir Charles and, via the trustees, Sebastian, were wealthy, all of us involved in the family's asset management needed to keep abreast of the times and run everything as commercially as possible within whatever constraints the family dictated.

White House was an interesting project. Normally when we had cottages to re-let, we simply re-let them. However, White House was a bit different because of its position and quality. It would likely appeal to people of some means provided that it offered a fairly high degree of accommodation. The colonel had managed for years with a rather antiquated central-heating system and only one bathroom, despite seven bedrooms. If we were to attract a high-paying tenant then an element of updating was required.

Once the colonel had moved out I went to have a close inspection of the house. He had maintained it in good order but it was very much a late 1960s or early 1970s house in feel. In particular the kitchen with orange-fronted and fake wooden Formica topped units was unlikely to appeal to the kind of tenant that I had in mind. So I drew up a list of works to be done which included a new bathroom, en suite to the main bedroom, a further second main bathroom, updated central heating, a new kitchen and redecoration throughout.

Unfortunately at the time the in-house estate building staff were busy with maintenance at the Hall and repair work on a number of village

240

cottages. To avoid waiting until the autumn, I invited three firms of local building contractors to quote for the work.

To begin with it was all straightforward. I drew some detailed scale plans and prepared a comprehensive specification of the works required. I asked Anne to find, by recommendation, three builders to come and have a look and provide us with a fixed quotation.

They duly made their appointments and I took each one of them to White House and showed them around. The quality of the personal recommendations, which I generally thought of as being better than merely leafing through the Yellow Pages, obviously varied.

The first two builders were competent and thorough. They followed my specification without hitch or much more than the occasional query. The third one was a different kettle of fish and I wondered whether he had been recommended by a slightly retarded, possibly even insane, supporter of a 'getting the community back to work' group. The builder himself certainly fitted that description and instilled as much confidence as a blind airline pilot.

I met him at White House early one Tuesday morning before most normal people were out of bed.

'Ahh,' he said, 'you'll be Sir Aden then, I suppose?'

'No, I'm Mr Aden,' I replied. 'I think you're confusing my name with Sir Charles Buckley, who owns the estate. I am his agent.'

He looked a little confused but said, 'Oh, I see,'

which I don't think he did.

'Anyway you must be Archie Trough,' I went on, 'so come on in and I'll show you what we have in mind.'

I noticed that he walked with a very pronounced limp and although he could have only been in his early fifties he had the demeanour of someone much older. I also happened to notice that he wasn't carrying any papers or, come to that, anything to write on.

'Have you brought the plans and specifications?' I asked.

'Oh, no, no,' he said, 'I never bring papers out on site. Trouble is I always lose them or they get covered in muck.'

'Oh,' I said, surprised. 'How are you going to remember what to price for?'

He tapped his head knowingly. A filthy trilby was perched on the top of it and I half expected him for a moment to raise it and produce a neatly folded copy of the paperwork that he had been sent.

However, that was not the case.

'Well, we'll start on the ground floor,' I suggested and led him into the kitchen. The whole room was to be ripped out and a modern design incorporated, which included replacing a solid-fuelled Rayburn with an oil-fired Aga.

Mr Trough entered the room and looked around in awe.

'My gawd!' he exclaimed. 'This is a big room, ain't it? I'll 'ave my work cut out just doin' this bit.'

'I wasn't really hoping you would say that,' I

commented. 'There's an awful lot more to do apart from the kitchen.'

'Is there, by gawd,' he said, clearly daunted by the prospect. I wondered what sort of building jobs he normally took on and was beginning to think that Mr Trough might be a waste of time. Nonetheless I showed him the other work necessary on the ground floor. Every room or job produced a number of 'my gawds' but still no notebook or evident means of recording the desired works.

Matters deteriorated, in fact they were concluded, when we reached the bottom of the main staircase.

'Right, well we'll have a look at the first floor now,' I told him, 'and in particular where we are going to install the new bathrooms.'

'Oh,' he replied, 'there's work to do upstairs, is there?'

'Well, yes, there is,' I retorted, somewhat annoyed. 'If you read or brought the plans you would have known that, Mr Trough.'

'I 'ave read 'em but I don't recall anything about being upstairs.'

'I can assure you that it does refer to upstairs; in fact more than half the work is upstairs.'

'Well, I've got a problem with that, I'm afraid, Sir Aden,' he remarked, back to bestowing a baronetcy upon me.

'And what is the problem with upstairs, Mr Trough?'

'I can't get there,' he explained, 'see, I don't do upstairs.'

I had been involved with builders on various

estates in my working life but I had yet to come across one that did not go upstairs.

'It's due to me leg, I can't get up the stairs.'

I looked incredulously at him. 'How do you get up ladders then?'

'I don't do ladders either. It was 'cos of the ladder that I did my leg in, see. I fell off a ladder that's done my hip in. Smashed it to smithereens it did.'

I stayed silent for a few moments, reflecting on a builder that couldn't use a ladder, but was interrupted by him carrying on, 'But I can stand on things you see.'

'What do you mean, stand on things?' I enquired.

'I can stand on boxes and little ramp things so I can reach the high bits. That's why I tend to do bungalows in the main.'

I felt Anne had a little explaining to do with regard to one of her recommendations.

'I think, Mr Trough,' I ventured, 'that this might not be a suitable job for you after all. Not unless you've got a partner or someone who'll be helping you with the work.'

'No,' he told me, 'I try to do all the work on me own, 'cos me partner's got a full-time job. She's a cook in the school at Bury.'

'I didn't mean that sort of partner, Mr Trough. I meant a partner in your business, or some workmen or subcontractors, something like that.'

'No,' he said proudly, 'I'm a sole proprietor, it's all me own business, you see.'

I could see, I could see quite clearly why no one would possibly entertain either being in partnership or working for this man who was, quite frankly, an idiot. Without more ado, and I have to admit with a considerable amount of irritation, I led him out of the house back to his van. I maintained my civility as best I could but was acutely aware that he had got me up early only to waste my time.

Chapter 19

The business with Mr Trough was coincidentally the beginning of a depressing trough in the life of the Frampton Hall Estate, in particular with Sir Charles.

I had been telephoned by Hole, mid-afternoon, in a terrible flap because Sir Charles had fallen off his horse. Hole did not get into flaps and so I took his concern seriously.

'Mr Aden, Hole here,' he had announced on the phone, 'I've some rather distressing news, which I would rather not impart over the public telegraphic system.'

This sort of thing was normal with Hole but when I suggested that his news might wait until the next morning when I was calling at the Hall anyway he would not have it and offered a partial explanation about the accident.

'Right then, I'll be up in about ten minutes,' I said, and finished what I was doing before explaining to Anne what had happened.

I drove up to the house in my appallingly filthy Land Rover, not so much concerned as to its condition but enjoying, as I always did, the wonderful scenery around me.

The thorn in the hedges was in leaf and the countryside looked that little bit greener after five months or so of dreary drabness. It was the annual promise of life to come. The grazing lands of the park had a green glow of young grass. Most of the trees were still bare but there was a definite awakening of the oaks, which, according to folklore, heralded a dry summer as the ash was still behind.

As usual I was met at the East door by Hole.

'You seem distressed, Mr Hole,' I said.

'I am, Mr Aden, I am,' he answered, 'and I have to say, Mr Aden, that I am distinctly worried about Sir Charles. In fact for the first time in my life I've gone against his orders.'

I looked at him quizzically. 'What have you done?'

'I'm afraid I've called the doctor, Mr Aden. Sir Charles wouldn't hear of it but I don't think he is at all well.'

'Can you tell me what has happened? I know you said he fell off his horse but is he badly injured?'

'Well, this is the trouble, Mr Aden, I don't think he's hurt as such but I suspect he's knocked his head or something. He doesn't seem to be making much sense and when I helped him up to his room he was talking about all sorts of things that happened years ago.'

'I see,' I said. 'Who was with him when this happened?'

'I believe he was out riding with one of the grooms, which is just as well because apparently when he fell off he was unable to get back on the horse. They had to send for the stud groom to fetch him.'

It did seem a little more serious than I had first thought.

'Do you think Sir Charles would like to see me?' I asked Hole.

'Well I don't know about that but do whatever you think best.'

I followed Hole through the labyrinth of passages up to Sir Charles' bedroom. He was lying semi-asleep in his magnificent four-poster bed in a room that was beautifully and elaborately decorated and so full of wonderful paintings and furniture that most people would have ignored the body lying in the bed and examined the contents of the room instead.

'Sir Charles,' I announced, 'I gather you're not feeling well. Fallen off your horse?'

'Who's that?' he asked.

'It's James Aden, sir,' I replied.

He tried to focus on my face.

'Ah, James,' he said weakly, 'I'm glad you're here. I had a bit of a fall today, came orf a horse, and Hole has been helping me out. I have to say I feel a bit queer.'

He looked dreadful.

'I think you must have hit your head or something, Sir Charles, you certainly don't look very well and Hole has called for the doctor.'

'Oh, I don't need a doctor,' he replied. 'I think a bit of rest and some jugged hare for dinner. A couple of glasses of claret and I'll be as right as rain.'

One had to bear in mind that Sir Charles was in his late seventies, and falling from a horse and hitting his head was likely to be of more consquence than if it had happened thirty years ago.

'Well it won't do any harm for the doctor to see

248

you, Sir Charles, and we are all quite worried about you.'

'I think it's time to get up now,' Sir Charles said. 'I'd quite like some bacon.'

I could understand why Hole had been so insistent that I attend and I drew him aside.

'Have you managed to get hold of Sebastian?' I asked him in a whisper.

'No, Mr Aden, I thought I should get hold of you first and you would know what to do.'

'Okay, I'll go and ring Sebastian because I think Sir Charles is suffering more than he is letting on.'

I took my leave and went down to Hole's pantry to use the telephone. I rang Sebastian's house. Serena answered.

'James Aden here, Serena. I hope you're well.'

'Fine, thank you; in fact I'm glad you've rung as it'll save me calling into the office today.'

'Well, I'm not in the office at the moment Serena, I'm at the Hall. Sir Charles has had a fall from his horse and I wonder if Sebastian's in please?'

'Oh, dear,' she said. 'Is he all right?'

'I'm not sure that he is very well, Serena,' I said. 'In fact I think he's slightly concussed. The doctor's coming up to see him but I thought I should let Sebastian know.'

'Okay, I'll tell him straightaway,' she replied. 'I expect he'll want to come up.'

In fact they both came up to see Sir Charles, by which time the doctor had already arrived. Hole and I left them all with Sir Charles and we waited in Hole's pantry for further news.

When the doctor came down he explained that Sir Charles had received a nasty blow to the head and was suffering from concussion. Although it wasn't life-threatening the doctor was concerned that there could be some internal damage and wanted Sir Charles to go to the hospital for a scan.

But Sir Charles would have none of it.

'Keep a very close eye on him, Mr Hole,' he said, 'and if there's the slightest change, any change at all, then ring me immediately. I'll call in this evening anyway.'

Sebastian and Serena came down shortly afterwards and must have received the same advice from the doctor. It was Serena who took charge and gave Hole various instructions. Sebastian, who was not a particularly practical man, drew me aside.

'I'm sure he'll be all right,' he said, 'bit of a blow that's all. Between the two of them,' and he nodded towards Serena and Mr Hole, 'they'll make sure he's all right. I've got to deliver a lecture this evening in Cambridge so perhaps you could keep Serena updated.'

I went back to the office and of course had to let the girls know what was going on. They all expressed concern as they were fond of Sir Charles and appreciated his generosity as an employer.

I remembered then that when I had telephoned Sebastian, Serena had answered the phone and she had wanted to talk to me about something. With Sir Charles' accident it had, understandably, slipped her mind. I rang and spoke to her.

'Serena, you wanted to tell me something, and

of course we forgot about it. Was it something urgent?'

'Oh, um, not really, but thank you for calling back, James. In fact it's rather sort of bad timing to bring it up. It was about our intended move up to the Hall.'

'Oh, yes,' I agreed, 'I don't suppose it's at all the right time to be bringing that up again with Sir Charles.'

The intended move, which involved father and son swapping residences, had initially been brought up by Sir Charles but somehow never progressed beyond discussion. Personally I felt that Sir Charles could see it was a sensible idea but couldn't quite bring himself to commit to the upheaval. It was understandable as he had lived there all his life and indeed it wasn't as if Sebastian and Serena were living in a tiny cottage. Bulls Place Farmhouse was superbly comfortable, luxuriously disposed and large enough to accommodate a sizeable family.

A move was psychologically the beginning of the end. It was a difficult balance to achieve. Sir Charles wanted to see Sebastian and Serena more integrated into the estate but he wanted to be sure of a smooth succession. Yet at the same time he was reluctant to give up the reins as Frampton was his life. There were various complicated trusts that meant Sebastian was more entitled to live in the Hall than his father but even so the various talks and discussions between the family and the trustees had come to nothing.

Life on the estate carried on as usual of course, the problems of the 'Big House' of no immediate consequence to the people of the village.

I was reminded of this as I stood in my office looking out of the window across the market-place. Robert Driscoll, a short man who reminded me of an English bulldog, was marching towards our door. That was until he opened his mouth and spoke with a high-pitched nasal whine, which somehow changed one's assessment of him immediately.

He was here for one thing only, and I knew that because it was the only thing he ever came to see me about.

I heard him barging through the estate-office door and could imagine him standing in front of Anne's desk, hands on hips, aggressively poised, chin thrust forward and then, 'I wonder if Mr Aden's there, please,' he squeaked.

'I'll go and see if he's available, Mr Driscoll,' Anne said. 'Have you made an appointment with him?'

'No, I haven't,' he replied. 'However, I was hoping he might be here.'

She came in to see me and closed the door behind her.

'Yes, I've already seen who it is,' I said to her. 'Frankly I don't want to see him because it's always a waste of time. But I suppose I'd better otherwise he'll just come back.'

'I'll show him through then,' she said and went to get him.

I had forgotten how short he was, maybe only a touch over five feet but, as if to make up for it, he shook hands with all the intensity of a piston driving an internal-combustion engine. He had a

252

vice-like grip so I was unable to let go of his hand even though I felt as though I was being pushed and pulled backwards and forwards across the room.

When he let go I almost catapulted into my desk. Having made his point, Mr Driscoll settled into the chair I offered him.

'I expect you know why I'm here,' he squeaked.

'Is it to do with Mrs Abraham's donkey?'

'I really think its time for the thing to go,' he said, sounding like a small child. 'The situation's getting worse and worse and if you don't do something about it this time then I'm going to call in the council.'

The root of the matter was that, for some particular reason, he hated donkeys and particularly the hee-haw sound they made. To some degree I sympathised because I also disliked the noise and it was beyond me why anyone should keep such a useless animal.

Mrs Abraham kept the donkey on a paddock rented from the estate, which ran behind her and Mr Driscoll's gardens. His annual visit to see me was always an attempt to persuade me that the matter was in estate hands – if we terminated her tenancy of the paddock then the donkey would have to go.

It wasn't something we were prepared to do, not only because it would have been unfair to Mrs Abraham and her donkey, but also because no one else in the vicinity had complained.

Although I didn't say so to Mr Driscoll I felt it was more of a psychological problem in that he probably compared his own stature to a donkey's,

253

rather than a racehorse's. Seeing and hearing the donkey every morning must have grated on his nerves.

So we had the usual squeaky discussion and, as we both knew it would, the matter was settled once again. Absolutely nothing would change.

What did happen, on an entirely different front, happened that evening.

For once I had left the office early and had been home in time to give Emma her tea. Afterwards, Sophie and I had spent the evening discussing the year's plans for the farm. The previous year with Emma's birth the farm had taken a back seat and pottered along with the Flatt brothers managing things in their uncomplicated way. But with Emma that little bit older and the able assistance of Mrs Painter in the house, Sophie wanted to start taking more of an interest again. She had a passion for the house and farm that stemmed from her childhood visits to Cordwainers when her Uncle William had owned the place.

We sat in the drawing room in front of a good fire in the inglenook and discussed all sorts of options to try to increase the farm's income. Basically it was an ordinary sheep farm with some arable and in all probability it would never be much else. Neither of us wanted to open any type of commercial venture which engaged the public, far from it, we liked the seclusion and privacy that it provided. But there were quite a few redundant farm buildings and it seemed a pity not to put them to some use. All the financially sensible options seemed to lead to having more people around. Conversion, either to offices or holiday cottages, was the obvious choices. You could see this all over the country where farmers were looking for increased income, but it always seemed such a shame to us to spoil one's splendid isolation.

What Sophie really wanted to do with the buildings was to house more horses and start a little stud. It was certainly a way to use them but not of increasing the farm income. In fact I could see an expensive hobby developing.

These were all just vague ideas and it was fun to live in such a place where one could have ideas and, on occasion, put them into practice.

In a relaxed frame of mind we went upstairs to our delightful bedroom with its ancient oak beams and elaborate four-poster bed. I thought back to when I had first met Sophie and she didn't seem to have changed a bit. As a student at the Rumshott Estate I had been struck by her beautiful features and long, dark hair. She still had a slim, fit figure and I curled up around her savouring the feel of her body against mine.

She rolled over and kissed me and we began to caress each other with gentle intimacy.

It wasn't late, just after 10 pm, when the phone rang. We looked at each other, slightly aghast, slightly amused.

'Who on earth can that be?' Sophie said. 'Nobody ever rings at this time unless it's urgent.'

Without answering her I picked up the phone.

'Mr Aden, it's Hole here. I'm sorry to ring you so late at night but I'm afraid Sir Charles has taken a turn for the worse.'

'What's happened?' I asked him.

'I'm afraid I've had to call an ambulance, Mr Aden. I think Sir Charles has suffered more than we first thought.'

'Has the doctor come over as well?'

'Yes, I summoned him at about 9 pm, Mr Aden. I went in to see Sir Charles then with his usual mug of Ovaltine and I couldn't wake him. So I called the doctor who came immediately and he asked me to get the ambulance, which is now here.'

'Have you rung Sebastian?'

'Yes, Mr Aden, I've done that and he and his wife are coming here now.'

'Well, thanks for letting me know, Mr Hole. I can come over if you or Sebastian would like, although there's not much I can do. I presume the ambulance will take Sir Charles to Bury hospital?'

'I believe so, Mr Aden. I think Sebastian is going over with him or following in his car, I'm not sure, but at least somebody will be there.'

'Thank you for ringing, Mr Hole. Could you let Sebastian know that we've talked, and if he wants to get hold of me, to ring, whatever time it is.'

Sophie had caught the gist of the conversation.

'I feel I ought to go over there really,' I said to her, 'but if Sir Charles and Sebastian have gone to the hospital then there's nothing I can do until the morning.'

'No, there's no point going,' she agreed. 'It's far better if you just stay here. If they need you they can phone you.'

It was difficult to get back to sleep so after a

256

restless half an hour I got up and went down to the kitchen and made some tea. Sophie had fallen asleep and I sat by the Aga, reflecting on the future at Frampton depending on Sir Charles' health.

The future became very uncertain. Sir Charles' fall had not only concussed him, but also caused some bleeding in his brain. He remained in hospital for a week but at his insistence returned to Frampton and we engaged a nursing agency to look after him.

Fortunately by early summer he was well again, but very much frailer and more forgetful. It was as though he had suffered a small stroke. He would certainly never be fit enough to ride his beloved horses again and he was not allowed to drive his car.

Hole became his shadow, following him around like a loyal dog. It meant that Sir Charles could do most of the things that he had always done but it was very distressing for everyone else to see how quickly he had deteriorated.

It also brought to a head the question of when Sebastian would move into the Hall. It was evident now, more than ever, that he really needed to be seen as the successor to this great landed estate and baronetcy. It would be an extremely delicate matter to instigate the move without making Sir Charles feel sidelined. However, his decision-making, in terms of the estate, had become so vague that practically everything was left up to me and I would then refer to either Sebastian or the trustees as necessary.

Sebastian clearly had a great academic mind but

lacked commercial intuition. Serena, however, showed more competence and I sensed that it would be her who would effectively take control when Sebastian acceded to the baronetcy.

There didn't need to be any formalities in the house changeover – on paper everything belonged to 'the estate'. All the bills for each house were routed to the estate office anyway so it was simply a matter of change of address cards and shuttling about moving personal possessions and the odd painting or piece of furniture. But emotionally the change was enormous and the week before it was due to take place, Sir Charles suffered a further blow to his health. It was nowhere near as serious or dramatic as before but he was advised to spend some time in bed and rest. The doctor also asked for a meeting with myself and Sebastian, where he made it abundantly clear that in his opinion Sir Charles' move from the Hall was out of the question. His view was that even though Sir Charles had agreed to the move it was distressing him and harming his health. Sebastian discussed the matter with Serena and they came to see me in the estate office.

A unanimous decision was taken that all the plans for their move would be put on hold indefinitely. It was not a particularly satisfactory state of affairs but the well being of Sir Charles was paramount.

The doctor was right. After that, Sir Charles regained some of his earlier composure, and although he appeared frail and his mind wandered he retained his passion for the Estate. He spent more and more time with his horses at the stud although he never expressed a desire to go riding.

It was sad to see a fit, energetic man decline so rapidly. Although he was approaching his seventy-seventh birthday he had never seemed, until now, to be anywhere near that age. Most people would have put him in his late sixties.

We re-started our weekly management meetings, which reinforced the old status quo. It was a relief, for both of us, to get back into a routine. The agenda also tended to remain the same although I did what I could to drag up items for discussion. Unbeknown to Sir Charles more major and long-reaching agenda items were left off but I brought them up with Sebastian and the trustees. Despite the house move being put off, there was an im-perceptible shift of balance with Sebastian heavily involved in major decisions. To some extent that was what Sir Charles had wanted for years, but his personality and intricate knowledge of the estate had unwittingly left Sebastian in the shadows.

Management meetings were always at 10.30 am on Wednesday mornings and I would arrive at the Hall to be greeted by Hole and shown to the study. Coffee and biscuits would be served, the poodles would behave badly and Sir Charles would sit opposite me across the fireplace.

As I had done for week after week, year after year, I sought topics to include on the agenda. On this occasion we had the following:

Date for the summer carnival.

The price of softwood sawlogs.

Shops – early closing.

Ferret allowance.

Any other business.

This was a typical agenda, and mostly straightforward, although Sir Charles continued to express his strong opinions on matters that concerned him.

Number one was simple in that the date had already been set for the carnival. Number two was more to his interest as he was interested in forestry and liked to keep abreast of news. I was able to report that the price of timber being sold from the estate had nearly doubled over the past twelve months.

Number three caused much more of a debate.

'Shops – early closing,' I said to him.

'Yes, I see,' he commented. 'What's all this about then?'

'Well, you may recall, Sir Charles, that in all our commercial leases for shops in the village there is a clause that insists that they close at 1 pm on a Wednesday.'

'Yes, yes, I know that,' he said, 'we've always had it. What's it on here for?'

'Well, there's a general consensus amongst our shopkeepers that it's not good for business to close on a Wednesday afternoon. They tell me that it's putting them at a disadvantage to other traders in Bury or the nearby villages.'

'Oh,' he said, 'but they've always shut on Wednesdays, ever since I can remember.'

'I know they have, Sir Charles,' I agreed, 'but times are changing and the Merchants Guild, which represents most of the village shops, has asked me to discuss it with you. They really feel it's affecting their businesses.'

'I thought all shops closed on Wednesday after-noons.'

Sir Charles did not, and had not as a rule, gone shopping very often. He went to London to see his tailor or shoemaker but ambling along the High Street was not his thing. I doubted whether he had been shopping in Bury St Edmunds since the 1960s, when quite possibly shops did close on a Wednesday afternoon.

'You know many shops are often open on a Sunday now, Sir Charles, let alone Wednesday afternoons.'

He sat bolt upright in his chair and stammered, 'I'm not having them open here on a Sunday. They should be at church.'

I wasn't sure if 'they' meant the customers or the shopkeepers. Probably it was both. One thing that was noticeable about Sir Charles since his health began to fail was that he tended to lapse into the past and dwell on a situation as it might have been decades earlier. It made discussions such as this quite difficult.

'I really would advise you, Sir Charles, to reconsider the Wednesday early closing, although you can still insist that nothing opens on a Sun-day.'

I managed to persuade him that it wouldn't be untoward to have the Frampton shops open all day on a Wednesday but he was still sharp enough to add, 'I think if they're open that bit longer then we can ask for an increase in the rent.'

I was about to reply with some non-committal statement when one of the poodles violently broke wind. In the formal setting of Sir Charles' library it was a little embarrassing and we might well have glossed over it but the wretched dog got up and started sniffing its bottom.

It got worse.

'Was that the dog?' asked Sir Charles.

I was momentarily caught off guard; surely he didn't think it was me.

'Well I had presumed so, Sir Charles,' I replied, which somehow didn't help. I was becoming detached from the reality of the moment and looking down at the scenario started to make me laugh, at least on the inside. It was one of those awful moments, the sort that sometimes one gets at a funeral or a moment of great seriousness, when a nervous giggle erupts into uncontrollable laughter. With a great deal of difficulty, and a huge amount of self-control, I directed his attention to item four on the agenda.

'Ferrets,' he said, 'what's this about then?'

'Really just to let you know that, erm, we're increasing the keepers' ferret allowance as from next month. There's a guideline that gets published each year and I thought you would like to know that.'

'Ah, very good,' he said, 'yes, that is good. Wonderful little things those ferrets. Didn't know we had many here actually but I suppose the men keep them, do they?'

'There's a few, Sir Charles, yes. I'm not sure how many but a dozen I suppose.'

'Oh,' he said, 'as many as that? Is this going to mean a lot more expenditure on our part?'

'No, Sir Charles, no. It's not really the money side that I was alerting you to because I think its only about 30p per ferret per week, or something, no it was just that I know you like to be kept informed, especially with anything to do with the shoot.'

'Ah, well, I see, yes, good. Well 30p, that's not too bad, is it? I'm quite happy to settle on that then, James. Now then, any other business?'

'No, I think that's all for this week, Sir Charles, but if anything arises urgently between now and next Wednesday then of course I'll let you know.'

With that I took my leave and returned to the estate office. It was good to know that despite the unrest of the past few months things were now returning to normal.

Chapter 20

Summer in the Suffolk countryside is sublime. The big open skies bring a clarity of light so revered that artists flock to the county. Most of them congregate along the East Anglian coastline like cockles clinging to the hull of a wooden boat but we had one such artist in Frampton, an eccentric woman in her early sixties with an unruly mop of dyed-orange hair. At least I presume it was dyed because I don't think such a colour could ever have been natural on a living animal. The nearest I could think of would be a tiger, but even they had a shimmering glow to their fur. This was an orange that shrieked at you with alarming fright. Her hair was a forewarning of her manner of speech as Ada Wilkinson usually shrieked at you.

Her husband Cecil was a meek man and between them they did a lot for the church. He was an honorary verger and helped dish out the hymn books and so on while she took delight in helping with flower arranging and cleaning the brass.

She also staged a twice-yearly exhibition of her paintings in the village hall, which she generously sold on behalf of the church. Everybody has their own tastes but whenever I had visited her exhibitions I wondered who on earth was buying her paintings. If she had given them to me as an honoured friend, they would have lived in the loft only to be brought down when she visited.

When the village hall entertained her exhibitions, the walls were covered with her work. They resembled nothing short of a catastophe.

One of Cecil's jobs was to mount and frame these things, which he did so most professionally. Uncharitably I suspected that most people bought the paintings because of that, and then replaced the painting with a photograph or some print that they had bought at a car boot sale. This is the only way I can explain how they all came to be sold. This was tremendous for the church coffers but less so for the inhabitants of Frampton. Privately I worried that the beautiful, medieval cottages of the town might be infested, aesthetically speaking, by the efforts of Ada Wilkinson.

Sir Charles, who was fairly frail by now, had accompanied me to a viewing. It was rather grandly announced as a private viewing, such as famous artists might have in Bond Street, W1, and was accompanied by a glass of wine together with a cube of cheese and a piece of tinned pineapple on a cocktail stick. For a lunchtime event it seemed somewhat meagre.

Sir Charles, who had become even more frank in his opinions, was not overly impressed. To be fair he did spend his days surrounded by Canalettos and Rembrandts, so Mrs Wilkinson did have some stiff competition.

She met us at the door when we arrived and was greatly honoured to have her work examined by the man she wanted to think of as her patron.

Fortunately there ensued a great deal of confusion over Sir Charles' comments. He walked into the hall and looked around him.

'Good Lord,' he said, 'did you create all this?'

To me the tone he adopted sounded as though he was speaking to a delinquent he had caught defacing a bus shelter, but Mrs Wilkinson did not appear to notice.

'Indeed, I did,' she replied and kept bobbing in a sort of curtsy, as though he was a member of the Royal Family.

Sir Charles looked at her as though he was worried that there was something wrong with her legs.

'Yes,' she gushed, 'I exhibit twice a year, Sir Charles, all in aid of the church you know. In fact I've got quite a reputation for my work.'

'I'm sure you have,' he replied dryly.

'And there's a special one I'd like you to see, Sir Charles,' she implored, 'of Frampton Hall. Maybe it's one that you would like to buy.'

She led us over to a painting that looked vaguely like a large sugar lump placed on a bed of lettuce. Its likeness to Frampton Hall in its parkland was about as close as Blenheim Palace is to a council house in Hounslow.

'Is that it?' said Sir Charles, pointing at the painting.

'Yes, it is, Sir Charles,' enthused Mrs Wilkinson, 'I've tried to capture the essence of its architectural merit within the natural undulations of our beloved countryside.'

Neither Sir Charles nor myself knew what to say without being rude.

'I certainly think it's got an element of the abstract about it, Mrs Wilkinson,' he agreed.

Mrs Wilkinson seemed pleased by the comment and bobbed up and down a bit more before showing us some more of her work. Some of them had little red stickers on them, which she proudly informed us meant that they had already been sold.

'Who the bloody hell would buy this stuff?' whispered Sir Charles to me.

There wasn't time to respond before Mrs Wilkinson had grabbed his sleeve and led him on to another collection, this time depicting views of the village.

Unless she had been sitting in a manhole studying the sewage system of the village, I could find no resemblance to the Frampton I knew.

'James,' murmured Sir Charles, 'I'm not feeling very well suddenly. Would you mind awfully taking me back to the Hall?'

I looked at him and noticed that he had gone very pale. With a brief goodbye to Mrs Wilkinson, who seemed somewhat taken aback by our rapid departure, I guided him out to the car.

When we got there he leant for a moment against the passenger door, supporting himself by holding on to the car.

'Are you all right, Sir Charles,' I enquired, concerned.

'I'm feeling a bit dizzy again,' he said. 'I'll be all right in a moment. No need to make a fuss.'

After a few moments he allowed me to open the door and help him into the seat. I drove him quickly back to Frampton Hall and enlisted Hole to help Sir Charles into the house. He was frail enough to need both of us to help him.

'Would you like to retire to your bedroom, Sir

Charles?' asked Hole.

'No, no,' Sir Charles replied very quietly, 'I want to go to my study. Is the fire lit, Hole?'

'Yes, sir, it's all ready as I was expecting you back in about half an hour anyway.'

'Very good, very good, then help me along.'

His dogs came to see him and instinctively knowing that he wasn't well, followed him closely as we led him to the study.

Once he was settled into his favourite armchair, Hole bustled off to make some tea.

'Thank you, James, I'll be fine now,' Sir Charles said. 'I think I need a bit of a rest and a cup of tea, and then I'll be fine. I think it was the sight of those bloody awful paintings that's brought this on you know. I know she means well but frankly I've seen better artwork in a public lavatory in a bus station.'

I laughed. At least he hadn't lost his sense of humour, nor his forthright manner.

I left him comfortable in his study and, with a tinge of sadness, reflected that I would never ride on horseback around the estate with him again. His frailty that day brought home to me how much he had aged in the past six months.

I drove through the parkland back towards the village and my office. It was a glorious afternoon and the rolling acres of Frampton Park were as heavenly as any place in England. The huge oak trees, centuries old, spread their mighty boughs as if holding out their arms to embrace life. They had done this for the 500 years the Buckley family had been guardians of the landscape. The lake was still, reflecting the skies like a mirror and a small herd of fallow deer were collected at the water's edge. I had to stop the car. These were the moments that made a land agent's job so agreeable.

Away from the bustle of office life, traffic, telephones and village peculiarities, even away from those that one held most dearly, such moments of inner calm and joy at the beauty and serenity of nature were to treasure.

As I gazed around the vista, not at all like Mrs Wilkinson's dreadful painting, I saw Sir Charles walk out from his study on to the south front and lean against the stone balustrade overlooking the park. I knew that he too would be having similar thoughts. For over half a century he had been the landscape's guardian, a responsibility that he took seriously and with great enthusiasm. A man of principles and high morality, he had spent so many years as a widower that his passion had become the estate and the desire to leave something for Sebastian to cherish.

I turned to climb back into the Land Rover but as I did so a pair of buzzards came into view, their distinctive cries penetrating the peace. I watched them circling for a few minutes and I could see Sir Charles doing the same from his vantage point on the terrace. Reluctantly, I drove back to my office.

Within the hour, Anne put through a call to me.

'Hole here, Mr Aden,' his voice quavering in distress. 'I have the most, I am in the most, I have the most dreadful news to impart. Our dear Sir Charles has passed away.'

I had been standing by my desk when I took the

269

call but I sat down with a thump in my chair. I didn't know what to say. My mind was racing, I'd been with him just an hour previously and although he had seemed frail this did not seem possible.

'I-I shall come straight away, Mr Hole,' I stammered and put the phone down.

I hadn't even thought to ask whether he had phoned Sebastian, but that could wait until I reached the Hall. It was strange but comforting that I should be so affected by this news. In a way it would have been what Sir Charles wanted. He loved people, his people as he put it, and for him to have known that his death would be sorely felt by those around him was a tribute to his command of his small empire.

In the days that followed I was engaged by Sebastian to organise arrangements. I felt deeply distraught that we had lost a good and kind man who cared for his community.

But underneath it all I had the unswerving conviction that it was the distress of seeing Mrs Wilkinson's bloody awful paintings that had killed him.

The publishers hope that this book has given you enjoyable reading. Large Print Books are especially designed to be as easy to see and hold as possible. If you wish a complete list of our books please ask at your local library or write directly to:

Magna Large Print Books
Magna House, Long Preston,
Skipton, North Yorkshire.
BD23 4ND

This Large Print Book for the partially sighted, who cannot read normal print, is published under the auspices of

THE ULVERSCROFT FOUNDATION